Old Love, New Life

To Evelyn, my friend

Old Love, New Life

by

Ruth Hays

Ruth Hays

DORRANCE PUBLISHING CO., INC.
PITTSBURGH, PENNSYLVANIA 15222

ISBN # 0-8059-5671-9

Printed in the United States of America

First Printing
For information or to order additional books, please write:
Dorrance Publishing Co., Inc.
643 Smithfield Street
Pittsburgh, Pennsylvania 15222
U.S.A.
1-800-788-7654
Or visit our web site and on-line catalog at www.dorrancepublishing.com

Dedication

This book is dedicated to all men and women over the age of fifty years who enjoy life to the fullest and love reading about places, people, and events that happened when they were young. This book is more than a love story. The elder citizens of a rural community can relate to the story line because it is life to them.

Chapter 1

Jeanette heard her name called. Searching over the crowd, she spotted her sister, Audrey, standing near a magnificent black stallion held in perpetual gallop on the most beautiful merry-go-round she had ever seen in her life. Just as she reached Audrey the merry-go-round began to move and the ride was started. Jeanette grinned at the audacity of her eight-year-old niece on the back of the black fury whose nostrils flared as if he would blow smoke and whose teeth bared as if he could make a quick turn and bite the child's leg. His mate beside him was identical in every respect, except white instead of black. Ree, her eight-year-old niece, astraddle the huge horse, clung to the pole with one hand and to the reins with the other, her feet dangling a good foot from the stirrups.

Turning to Audrey, Jeanette asked, "Why in the world did Ree choose such a large mount when there are those lovely palominos which aren't at all fierce looking?"

Audrey laughed, "Ree picked the horse herself." Ree was the nearest thing to a boy her mother and dad were to have. She was all tomboy from the very beginning.

Before meeting Audrey, Jeanette had been idly strolling through the park. She hadn't been to the Corn and Stalk Show in over twenty years. The three-day celebration was an annual event much looked forward to by the people in the rural community of Queen City, Missouri. Thursday through Saturday programs for entertainment had been arranged as well as judging of live-stock, best of crafts, home prepared foods, quilts, rugs, canned goods, etc.

Jeanette could remember the excitement she herself once felt as a teenager, marching with the school band in the parade, always held on Saturday afternoon at 1:00 P.M. Every marching band from all schools within the county were there to strut their stuff, plus a few bands from outlying surrounding communities. This year would be no different. The band concert following the parade often lasted until 3:00 p.m. when the baby contest took place. Always there would be twenty-five to forty babies entered, all adorable, for the judges to look at and coo over. What a job to pick first, second, and third place winners. Judging a baby contest was one job Jeanette knew she could never perform.

The small park in the center of the town square was filled with happy, roaming people. The carnival, with its various rides for tots to oldsters, was doing a thriving business. The little-cars merry-go-round had every car full. There was a small train that followed a track around the perimeter of the park. She heard the toot-toot and the delighted squeals of the kiddies as the small engine came around the curve. Every seat was taken. She glanced at the ticket window and was amazed to see the children's rides were forty-five cents. They had only been ten cents when her children had been that size. Still, in a span of thirty years that actually wasn't so bad, considering inflation in this day and age.

There was a real live pony-go-round, beautiful Shetland ponies slowly going around in a roped off circle, the grass completely gone where their little hooves had beaten a path in the three days they had been there. Jeanette smiled as she noticed one little boy doing his best to make his pony go faster. The child was perhaps four or five years old and plainly this was not the first time he had ridden a horse. He reminded her of Ree, her niece. When she was only three years old her father had taken her into the fields with him and let her ride the big tractor. In spring plowing time she would follow him behind the plow carrying an old coffee can which she plopped fishing worms into, as the plow would turn over the black soil. This was good ground, fertile ground, and except for one year when the river overflowed its banks, Lee had received a high yield of whatever crop he had planted. He was a smalltime farmer compared to some of the big acreage growers but he had worked hard and done well. His small Black Angus herd had multiplied through the years until now it was worth close to twenty thousand dollars. The beefers were to be used as funds for sending the two older girls through college, but already part of that dream was dying.

Audrey continued telling all this to Jeanette as they waited for Ree to finish her ride. Velma was only seventeen. She would not be eighteen until January and would graduate from high school in the spring when school was out in May. Audrey had known for some time that Velma had no interest in going to college, but she had hoped she would at least take a business course at the local junior college or even attend one of the trade schools. But Little Miss Velma had other ideas. She wanted to get married. In fact, she wanted to get married now. Audrey had a deep fear inside her that the girl was doing something very foolish and in fact may *have to* marry before the agreed upon June wedding date. Somehow, her oldest daughter was drifting from them. Now, she began to explain to Jeanette, the more she thought about it, the more she realized it wasn't a sudden change. From the very beginning Velma had been adverse to the farm. Even as a little girl she never liked to be around the animals, rarely went near the barn. Audrey would carry her through the muck in the barn lot and put her in a clean manger, a manger in which she kept an old quilt so the straw would not chafe Velma's delicate skin. As she grew older she took over more and more of the housework in deference to outside chores. She didn't mind the canning as long as she didn't have to pull it or pick it. When Velma was twelve years old she could plan and prepare decent meals, her baking measured up to an average adult, and she could cut out and sew a complete wardrobe. Already she was dabbling in light make-up and was called by her sister Janie, "Miss Priss Clothes Horse." Audrey reflected that no two sisters could be any more different. Janie had come along a scant thirteen months on the heels of her sister. It wasn't planned that way but both Audrey and her husband Lee accepted things as they came, and both loved and reveled in their babies. The girls never lacked for love or understanding. Even discipline was fairly administered. Velma was a petite, dark-haired image of her mother, whereas Janie favored the Willis's. Lee Willis was big, brawny, and very, very blond. Janie was blond and large-boned for a girl. Her hair was straight and hung loosely down her back. Sometimes for special dress-up occasions her mother would arrange her hair to softly curl about her face. She was pretty in a wholesome, hardy way.

And now the whole family was here at the Stock Show. It was as gala as any state fair, only on a smaller scale. Janie had entered her Future Farmers of America calf and had received a red ribbon. She also had been offered a substantial sum for him but at this point Pedro was not for sale. Janie, in pig-tails and jeans, had scarcely left the calf's side since her father unloaded early Thursday morning.

She had curried and combed and cleaned and softly sung to quiet the animal's nervousness in being in new surroundings. Pedro was her first exhibit in the show and though she didn't expect to take any ribbons she was never-the-less proud of her accomplishment. She was elected FFA Queen by her classmates at school and rode on the FFA Float in Saturday's parade. It was the only time she had worn a dress all week. She much preferred jeans or shorts with halter-tops of big loose pullover shirts. Often she would run around barefoot, forgetting where she had left her shoes. When the judges announced the winner in the calf competition Janie was over-joyed to hear Pedro, her Pedro, had taken second place.

Other teenagers in the competition were as pleased for her as if they themselves had won. And this Jeanette thought was what it was all about.

She said as much now to her sister: teamwork, fellowship, and sportsmanship. She had seen it all in the three days she had been with these kids. No juvenile delinquents here, though some of the pranks they played on one another were a bit frightening.

When Janie had informed her parents she planned to stay in town during the entire show her mother was aghast. A boy, of course, but a sixteen year old girl? Never! And Lee backed up his wife. Queen City wasn't even the town she attended school in, nor was it the town near their farm where she had grown up. Even acknowledging the fact that FFA leaders and sponsors would be on the grounds at all times, plus a security patrol hired special by the town council, even then Lee did not relish releasing the girl on her own. She begged, pleaded, even cried, but her folks stood firm in their decision.

After the chores were done, Mom or Dad would drive her thirty-eight miles into Queen City and leave her all day. Each evening after chores they would return and stay as late as 11:00 P.M. taking all three girls home with them. That was as far as they agreed to go.

Then on Sunday Jeanette had arrived, driving her pickup camper, and planning to vacation with relatives and friends for approximately three weeks before returning to her job in Phoenix, Arizona. It was her annual visit to the old home place. Audrey was her only sister and although she spent most of her vacation with their aged mother in Glenwood, she still managed several overnight visits in the homes of Audrey and their two brothers.

Jeanette was a widow. Her husband had passed away three years prior after a long and lingering illness. Jeanette was an accountant with a large business firm in Phoenix. She had been with the firm over twenty years and diligently worked hard, and her loyalty had earned her the respect of her peers. She started out with the firm as a secretary. At that time she had two small children in kindergarten and second grade. Husband Ed was a mechanic, a civil service employee, stationed at nearby Luke Air Force Base.

Jeanette was ambitious and energetic and was determined to get her degree in business despite her husband's disapproval. He felt she had her place in the home, caring for her family. He realized her salary was needed to supplement the family income but he was always resentful that his wife had to work outside the home. He was most belligerent when she expressed her desire to continue her formal education. Jeanette, however, had a way of overriding him when she really wanted something bad enough.

Jeanette was strong-willed, independent, healthy, and far too much woman for her husband to manage. He would bully her verbally, but in his heart he was just a little afraid of the pretty redhead he had wooed and wed. He even admitted it once to his brother.

Jeanette had her home and her job in sunny Phoenix. When her husband passed away her sons tried to persuade her to take an apartment, sell the house and the truck, but she had hung on to both. She drove the car to work but enjoyed the pickup and camper for vacations, short trips, and weekend camp-outs. She retained her membership in various organizations she and Ed had belonged to for so many years. Sometimes on club outings she would take her teenage grandsons.

Lary and Gary were fourteen now, twins by birth but as different as day and night. She had so much fun with her grandchildren. Joey was twenty-five and hadn't been married as long as Lin, but they had started a family almost immediately with baby Peter joining the family a scant year after their marriage. Ed worshipped this baby. He seemed to have a closer relationship with little Pete than he had had with Lin's children or his own sons for that matter. He spent more time with Petey and had more patience with him than with any of the other, almost as if he knew their time together would be so short.

Ed had suffered from asthma since birth. That was why they had eventually left their home in north Missouri for the drier climate of Arizona. He seemed to thrive in the summer heat. The sun boiled nearly everything it touched but Ed felt better than he had felt in years. Even his arthritis was less painful in the hot weather.

After twenty years in Arizona Ed began having trouble breathing once again. There were bad times when he would gasp for breath and nights he was unable to sleep at all. Then he developed a kidney infection that never did completely clear up. His feet and legs would swell until he was unable to get his boots on. His stomach began to expand and his neck and throat and face swelled. Doctors couldn't control it. He endured so many pills and shots and still had very little relief, which was only temporary at best. When his illness reached the point he was missing more days of work than he was there and his employer never knew from day to day whether he'd show up next day or not, Ed knew it was only a matter of time before he would be told by the shop foreman they'd have to let him go. So at the recommendation of the shop Union Stewart he applied for medical retirement.

After nearly three months of negotiating, his retirement finally was approved. His retirement check would only be about one-third as much as a paycheck per month. By now Jeanette would help him dress in the morning before she left for work and more often than not he would sit around the house in socks, unable to get his boots on and too stubborn to wear house slippers. It was difficult for him to get in and out of the car and they rarely went anywhere anymore. Fortunately, the kids lived in a nearby city and could come and go several times a week to help out and every day would call on the telephone. Friends called often but still he became despondent. He was cross with her for no apparent reason on her part and yet Jeanette knew it was frustration and pain that made him so, and she was patient and tried to understand.

The last year that his illness went from bad to worse the entire family lived under a tense dark shadow. Ed was in and out of the hospital so often it was easier to care for him at home than to constantly drive back and forth. She took a three month leave of absence to be with him and one morning early she awoke to find him sitting up in bed holding his throat, his fight for breath a choking gasp. She immediately began massage but in a matter of minutes he went limp in her arms. It was over. With a calmness only God could have given her, she gently laid him back on the bed and getting up and groping for her robe she called her two sons. Both boys were there within one-half hour. She had made a fresh pot of coffee, called the doctor, and dressed for the day. The doctor arrived shortly after the boys. She couldn't cry and she sat back silently while her sons and the doctor made all arrangements. She never moved out of the chair when the undertaker came.

After a week of rest she returned to work. It was blissful peace to come home to a quiet house. She would putter in the garden and yard, baby-sit with her young grandson, but never did she grieve for her lost husband. Somehow she had lost all the love she once had for him; only compassion remained. At one time he was her everything. But the years of ill disposition and constant nagging had eventually taken their toll on her affection and truth of the matter, he had literally bitched his way right out of her heart. Still she had good memories and remained true to her husband till the day he died. She had taught herself to live without love or at least she felt she no longer needed man to fulfill her comforts and interfere with her life.

Jeanette came and went at her own will. Now, here she was smack in the middle of a rural celebration, the annual Corn and Stock Show in her old home county.

She had arrived Sunday, smack in a heated debate between her niece and her parents. As she parked the truck she could hear loud voices coming from the kitchen. There was anger in the tone of voice, and Jeanette recognized the voice as her gentle brother-in-law's. She had never before heard him raise his voice either to Audrey, the children, or even the animals that resided on their farm. What on earth had happened? Jeanette was thinking perhaps she had arrived at a wrong time. She would leave before they knew she had arrived and return later. She could always drive into town and visit Aunt Stella who was now living in the Alcott Nursing Home.

Too late: She had hesitated too long. The porch screen door banged open and then banged shut and Janie came flying out. Unable to hold back her tears of frustration she nearly plowed right into the side of the camper in her mad dash to escape the house and those inside.

Jeanette took the girl in her arms and held her gently for some time until the sobs subsided.

"Now, tell me what has happened. Whatever is wrong, child? I heard the loud voices as I drove up."

"Not here Aunt Jeanette," and she nodded toward the meadow nearby and a newly stacked haystack of freshly mowed hay. Silently, Jeanette followed the girl to the other side of the haystack, and she mentally noted that they were now out of sight of the house. Falling down on the loosed hay at the base of the stack, Jeanette inhaled a deep lungfull of the sweet smelling clover.

"Now talk, start from the beginning. I want to hear it all."

Chapter 2

Janie began telling of her work in school and her pure enjoyment with the Future Farmers of America program. More and more, girls were becoming involved until now the FFA classes outnumbered the home economics classes in female membership. Pedro was hers from the very beginning, right from the day he was born, and Janie had resumed full responsibility for his welfare as soon as it became evident his mother was refusing to let him suck. There was no apparent reason why the cow rejected her calf and it was most unusual. Lee had never seen it happen before, but he had read of such an occurrence once in his stock journal. At first it was feared the calf would starve for lack of nourishment but Janie was patient and she prayed a little too. She had bottle-fed lambs in the past, why not a calf? Already she had named him "Pedro." He was being obstinate about taking to the nipple and no amount of coaxing would induce him to drink from a pail. Janie wanted to laugh at the picture of the poor little coal-black critter, more legs than body, with white foam all over his face where she had forced his head down into the bucket of warm, slightly sweet milk. She was almost positive he had not swallowed one drop. She had a bottle of warm milk and bucket of warm milk and somehow she must get some inside the little baby. This was the second day and he was visibly somewhat weaker.

Suddenly she was angry and in frustration, losing her patience and suddenly dipping her hand in the pail, she shoved her wet milk hand into the calf's mouth. His tongue licked her hand. Putting her hand back in the milk pail she again stuck her hand in the young mouth. This time there was a definite tug on her fingers and after a few more successful dipping and sucking she thrust the nipple in, instead of her fingers. Laughing and crying at the same time she stayed on the job until the Pepsi bottle had been nearly emptied and Pedro began to push the bottle away, refusing to take anymore. No matter. He had eaten. He would live now and grow strong and big. She knew it. She picked up the bucket and returned to the house by way of the corncrib where Old Blue was keeping close watch over her five little blue puppies.

Old Blue was a pureblooded bluetick hound. She was the finest bitch Lee had ever owned and she held her own on the trail of a coon. At night when the men and hounds traipsed over hill and dale, more often than not it was Blue heading the pack. All this Jeanette had heard before, but she listened quietly without interruption as the girl continued to unfold her tale. At least she wasn't crying now, and after all she had instructed her to begin at the beginning, hadn't she?

Janie poured the leftover milk into Blue's food pan. The milk was no longer warm but Old Blue didn't seem to mind. She began to lap up the milk, delighted at the extra treat, as Lee had not yet stopped by with her can of food. The puppies were still nursing and though now their eyes were open, they still depended solely on their mother for their livelihood. Picking up a fat little blue butterball of fur, Janie murmured, "It's a good thing, Blue, you didn't desert your babies." The puppies had never been outside the corncrib but Janie had heard her father, a day or so ago, that he must take Blue and her family to the barn soon to visit Blooper. Blooper and Blue were registered blueticks. Both were four years old and this was Old Blue's second litter. Each time she had had five puppies and each time all had lived. Usually, litters ran from seven to ten but Lee was satisfied since Blue was a good mother and had plenty of milk to feed five. There seemed to be no runts in either litter. They had sold every pup as soon as weaning was over for twenty-five dollars a pup and Lee had buyers for this group. However, he favored Tillie and had almost made his mind up to keep and train her for himself.

All this came pouring forth from Janie's lips as fast and as smooth as if someone had pulled the stopper out and turned the overflow loose. Finally she arrived to the current situation where she and Pedro were ready for their first show and she was batting zero in getting her folks to permit her to stay in town.

She could not trust Pedro to behave for strangers in her absence. Suppose he got loose and got hurt. The makeshift barns were near the highway and should he get loose a big truck might hit him. He was so big and so black he presented a frightening aspect to someone who should unexpectedly come face to face with him, someone who did not know him as she did. And Pedro himself was bound to be nervous and very well might hurt someone accidentally. So her pleas and her arguments went on.

Mr. Fisher and his wife would be camping on the grounds along with most of the FFA class; some in tents some in campers. Mr. Fisher was their teacher. Mrs. Fisher had even invited the girls to share a communal tent for sleeping. They would eat at the food stand operated by the Jaycees and their wives. Still Audrey and Lee felt the Fishers would have more than enough to do without the responsibility of one more young girl to look out for. And Janie had never stayed away from home overnight except in the company of relatives. And for three days and nights? Impossible! Absolutely unthinkable! So thought Audrey.

"Please, Aunt Jeanette. Can't you talk to Mother? Please try to make her see how much this means to me. Please?"

Jeanette agreed she would speak to Audrey. Already a plan was forming in her head that she did not wish to discuss with Janie until she had received approval to carry it out if indeed approval was received. Not wanting to raise her hopes only to have them dashed down again she would wait until she heard the opposition out before making her pitch. The two got up and walked together toward the house.

Seeing her mother coming toward them Janie made a hasty about-face to gather the eggs, she said. Apparently she was not yet composed enough to face her mother. After witnessing her mad departure from the house, Jeanette could feel empathy for the girl. She knew she was feeling a bit ashamed for her outburst as well as deeply hurt at the same time.

"Hello! Hello! When did you get here?" The sisters embraced and each exclaimed how well the other looked.

"Been talking to Janie, I see." Audrey hadn't missed her sudden veering away and suspected she was doing so purposely, probably to avoid a direct consultation with her. She wondered what conversation had taken place between the two and where. It was over an hour since she spotted the camper in the driveway and unable to stand it any longer had gone outside. She had looked in the cab and knocked on the camper door. Somehow she had a feeling that Janie was with her aunt and a sixth sense warned her not to call out. Pedro was standing in the lot swishing flies. She was just starting toward the barn, thinking perhaps the hayloft was harboring the duo for she felt certain they were together.

The big old maple tree in the corner of the yard provided shade for man and dogs, only now it was women and dogs. "So that's where they've been," Audrey thought to herself. Jeanette held a frisky pup in her arms. Spotting Audrey she had released the pup, who was not at all pleased at being picked up by this stranger and scampered away immediately. The other pups had all gone to new homes but Wendy was kept behind. She had not yet begun her training and unlike Blooper and Old Blue had the run of the farm. She was going to tag along Lee and Old Blue before she left the homestead. She was too young to take on the hunt but Lee thought by spring she would follow Blue and the pack without question or diversion.

Once he had started a young dog out too early and the dog left the pack to chase a rabbit. Becoming separated, and naturally curious, he wandered farther away, until finally he was lost. The men had searched and called nearly all night. All the other hounds returned but it was to be ten days before "Ga-Bo" found his way back to the familiar farmhouse. He was a sad looking creature, gaunt and muddy and limping badly.

Lee did not wish to lose a valuable dog like Wendy, so he was taking no chances in timberland and coonland before the dog was able to forage for herself. So Wendy stayed close to the house, seldom leaving the yard and going to the barn only when the humans did and returning likewise. Once Audrey had seen her chase a gopher in the garden. Audrey was really surprised when Lee kept Wendy. She had thought Tillie was the one he would keep. Out of the five puppies, three males and two females, Tillie was the one he would keep. Out of the five puppies, three males and two females, Tillie had been the one he most fussed over and she thought his favorite.

Sitting at the kitchen table drinking freshly made coffee, the two women began to discuss the situation at hand. Jeanette could well understand the paternal feeling to protect the young. She could also see Janie's side. After all, she would not be adrift among strangers in a pagan land. She would be only eighteen miles from her hometown and actually thirty-eight miles from her home. Her folks would attend each night and the school sponsors sounded like excellent chaperones. Then she dropped her own bomb.

"Would you like her to go with me? I understand there is an area on the premises set aside for campers, trailers, tents, etc."

"But that area will be filled mostly by carnival people. You don't want to sleep beside that lot."

"Oh Audrey, be reasonable. The people working in a carnival are just people like you and me. Their jobs are different from yours and mine but that doesn't mean that they are all crooks, rapists, murderers, etc. Chances are they are decent folks earning a living in a profession they enjoy. Looking back to previous carnivals I've attended the business was always booming unless rained out. Outside of packing up and moving on to a new location every few days the job should be fun. Even the moving from place to place is interesting. Not a business for a family with school age kids of course, though the summers could be fun and educational as well, I'd think."

Audrey still was not sold on the idea. "You don't know how it is. You only had boys to contend with. Girls are different. Lee says you need a tighter halter on girls."

"Surely you don't feel children can be treated in the same manner as horses?" She personally thought the whole idea was ridiculous.

"But, not at all, Jeanette. I don't think so at all, but Lee says women and kids can be managed in very much the same way and *he* believes it." He even practiced what he preached and for the most part secretly felt it worked. His family and his animals were happy and well adjusted as a whole. Lee's wife knew and understood him very well.

During the preparation of the evening's meal Jeanette and Audrey talked of many things but always the topic kept coming back to Janie and her dilemma. Audrey was beginning to weaken a little. She trusted her sister and knew Janie would indeed be well looked after under Jeanette's watchful eye and care. Perhaps if her father agreed, peace and harmony could once more be restored to the Willis household.

Chapter 3

The Willis supper table had long been a sounding off place for the entire family. Family matters were discussed in length and every member had a part. Usually when guests were present there was more small talk and less family talk. Lee believed families should take care of their own, regardless of what the problems might be, and one did not air their personal life before all and sundry but handled things concerning their own family privately whenever possible. In a small rural community people knew too much about other people as it was.

Tonight the meal started off on a cheerful, happy note and yet Jeanette could actually feel a tense atmosphere around the table despite the gay chatter. Dinner consisted of breaded pork chops, gravy, fried potatoes, sliced tomatoes, and glazed carrots, with a side dish of tossed salad, all homegrown products from their own farm. Jeanette buttered a hot biscuit and tasted the fresh butter Audrey had churned only that morning. She had a mental figure in her mind what a meal like this would cost in a Phoenix restaurant for six people. Of all the states she had traveled, Arizona still was the most expensive when it came to eating out. When you had to purchase every bite you ate, groceries could run into quite a sum. That was why she herself always kept a small garden in her backyard. She mentioned this and was told by a smug Lee that they raised ninety percent of their own food. Even in times when money was scarce they never had gone hungry. Audrey went on to say she had either frozen or canned nearly five hundred jars of fruits and vegetables this summer. The freezer in the kitchen was over half full of red raspberries, blackberries, boysenberries, gooseberries, dewberries, strawberries, fresh-cooked summer apples, summer squash, rhubarb, cherries, corn on the cob, as well as several pints of whole kernel corn and even several cartons of mixed vegetables for winter vegetable soup. She had pressure cooked and sealed in jars small whole Irish potatoes, succotash, green beans, shell beans, yams, and had over one hundred jars of pickles; bread and butter pickles, dills, sweet and sour, lime, and fourteen-day, not to mention all the jams and jellies on the shelf. Peaches had not done as good this year and the whole crop had been eaten already or given away to relatives. She had prepared six freezer pies and sealed six pints of pickled clings.

The late frost had hurt the three peach trees when they were just budding out. There weren't as many blossoms this year and the birds had taken their toll from the ripe fruit. The freestone was a young tree started from a sprout Lee had transplanted a few years back and probably wouldn't bear heavy for several years yet. Audrey went on to say some seeds thrown out in the chicken yard had sprouted up and now were waist high. The hens often sat in their shade but had not seemed to damage the young shoots. She wanted to start a small peach grove at the opposite end of the apple orchard. Nursery trees cost such a fortune that she felt like she should nurture and protect what God had given them free. Of course she had no way of knowing whether the sprigs in the chicken yard were clings, the small yellow peaches or freestones, the larger golden peach with red inside around the seed, but peaches were peaches and the smaller ones were put into jars and butters or pickled whole. The larger ones were halved and put up in quart Mason jars in heavy syrup, to be cold packed or open-kettle cooked.

Jeanette knew the routine well. She had done her share before moving to Arizona back in the early fifties. In fact she still missed the harvest season and gardening more than anything else she had left behind when she left her old home and ventured out to a strange land with a young husband and two small children. City life had never captured her heart as the country had. She still had a small garden, but it wasn't the same compared to the large truck patch she used to put out.

Velma got up to clear away the plates and bring in the dessert and Janie arose to assist her. All during the meal no one spoke about the upcoming show. The old plum tree had yielded a fine crop of prune plumes and Velma had baked a plum cake. She was also experimenting in drying some. Now as she cut the cake and Janie passed the serving plates to each person Velma began telling her aunt that the tin roof over Lee's tool shed was completely covered with plums, apples, grapes, and peaches drying. The cheesecloth cover was weighed down here and there with rocks and pieces of old brick to keep the fruit from blowing off and also to deter the birds from helping themselves. They had tied tin cans on a rope across the whole mess to make noise to scare away birds and even squirrels. The green gage plum and the large Sasuma prune plum were very good dried, the home economics teacher had told the class, and having both at home Velma was determined to try her luck. The peaches and apples were processing as expected but not having seen dried plums Velma was uncertain whether her batch was on schedule or not. They looked rotten to her and not the least appetizing. The

14

plum cake was delicious and was eaten without any topping. Finally, unable to stand it any longer, Jeanette turned to Lee and casually asked if he was planning on entering the tractor pulling contest this year. Most farmers in the area signed up for the various contests involving their farm machinery and skills. Lee replied in the affirmative. Last year he signed up but was unable to compete because his tractor had broken down. He never tried to compete every year but those years he did he always come into the top money. Two years ago he had taken first place. First place was a hundred dollars; second, fifty dollars; and third, twenty-five dollars. He sometimes competed in the chain saw contest too, but never had won in that event and did not plan to enter this year.

"Janie tells me she has an entry in the FFA exhibit. I think it is a wonderful gesture by the schools to encourage young people nowadays in farming." She smiled when she spoke but never took her eyes from her brother-in-law's face. Suddenly the room became so quiet you could have heard a pin drop and the tension you could cut with a knife. Lee glanced first at his wife and then looked long and hard at his daughter before turning back to face his sister-in-law. When he spoke his voice was controlled. The lopsided grin did not soften the grim expression around his mouth and eyes.

"I see you are aware of the situation here. You have probably heard that Janie wants to stay in town. In case you are of a mind to plead her case, don't. As a parent you must realize that the very idea in itself is absurd. Her mother and I have already agreed to take time out to make the round trip twice a day. Now, she will just have to abide by that."

A glance at Janie and Jeanette saw the girl was close to tears once again but was doing her best to bear up. Another five minutes and her composure would be shot to pieces. Already her shoulders were beginning to tremble and her lips quivered slightly. Taking the bull by the horns was not a new trick for Jeanette. She had always been independent and nervy. Her mother once told a friend that Jeanette would plunge in with her eyes open and both fists swinging when even the angels would back away. It was now or never. She would have her say regardless of the outcome. Still she knew she must choose her words carefully. Lee Willis was no Ed. Here was a man to be reckoned with. She had a deep respect for her sister's husband.

Smiling shyly she gazed directly into the eyes of the big blond man. Gently, almost demurely she chided, "Lee Willis, wipe that scowl off your handsome face. No one is trying to usurp your authority over your own children. But, yes, I have been talking with Janie, and I have been informed of the current situation as it stands now. And I just may have a solution to the problem. Now before you say *no* will you first at least hear me out?"

Lee noticed the stubborn chin tilt up and the steady gleam of her eyes as she squared off for battle. Now that he stopped to think about it he had seen that same look, that same expression on Janie, time and again. God, what a challenge a woman like that would be to a man. He had always loved

Audrey. Always would. But there were times he felt she gave in too easy. They never had had a real serious quarrel because she always seemed over-powered by his masculine strength and the fact that she was brought up to obey her father and then her husband could have something to do with it. Hard to realize that two sisters had the same father and mother, they were so different, and yet he knew they were alike in many ways.

Unable to remain angry his body relaxed and so did his facial expression. In his usually quiet way of speaking he told Jeanette he would not promise a yes or no to her proposition, but he would hear her out. Apparently they would all hear what she had to say for no one made a move to leave the table. She made her pitch fast. She promised to look after the girl personally, never letting her out of her sight, day or night. The camper was secure and comfortable. It could sleep six so two beds would be no trouble at all. She was even willing to take another girl if that would make Janie more at ease. The camper was equipped with a full kitchen facility and a small toilet and shower. All were self-contained, even electricity. She would have a ball and enjoy it as much or more than the kids.

"So what do you think? Am I or am I not a decent enough woman that you would trust the care of your daughter to me for three days and nights?" Put to him like that Lee acknowledged he was on the spot.

Janie squealed and jumped up and hugged her Aunt Jeanette, nearly dumping her half-filled coffee cup in her lap. Ree caught the cup before it slid off the table.

Ree was on her feet now. "Can I go too? Can I go too?" In her excitement her words ran together. Lee knew Jeanette's offer did indeed put a new light on the subject, and he did understand his daughter's feelings. It was exactly what he would want to do under similar circumstances. Had Janie been a boy he would not have hesitated giving his approval.

"All right! Quiet down, all of you. I haven't said any of you can go. Thank you Sis for the offer. I'll think about it. Audrey and I will talk it over and we'll tell you our decision in the morning." So saying, he excused himself from the table and went into the living room and turned on the TV for the six o'clock news.

Janie didn't think she could wait until morning. For the first time she really began to hope, but her father seldom relented when he had made a decision against something. He wasn't a man to back down after he had given his word. If he said *no* he meant *no* and further arguing only got her into trouble she knew from experience.

Jeanette had arrived in Glenwood only that morning. He mother was busy caring for a sick neighbor so she could not have a close homecoming chat as they usually did upon her arrival. Mother was eighty-two years old, a retired nurse, but she still went into homes all over town when needed. She no longer drove her car but she could walk for miles and never tire. When any of the townsfolk were ill they were more apt to call Grandma

Mary instead of a doctor. Doctors nowadays seldom made house calls and it cost a fortune when they did. There was a clinic in town but so many of the elderly had no transportation to get up town and they came to rely on their telephones and Mary.

Mary was grateful. As a widow with her children married and living away, her nursing duties kept her active, happy even. She did wish the children and grandchildren would come to see her more often. They lived busy lives of their own she knew, but it seemed like the babies were growing up so fast they hardly knew their grandmother. It had been ages since any of the grandchildren had stayed all night with her. She had a longing to hold their soft cuddly bodies and Ree was her partner in checkers. She came the most. But of course Audrey only lived twenty miles away. The others were scattered. And she had never yet seen Jeanette's grandbaby, her great grandchild. Joey hadn't been to Missouri since he first brought his bride to see her. Wilbur was living in California. They had been home on leave only three times in the past ten years. His three children were actually strangers, despite their letters and pictures exchanged over the years. Wilbur's oldest daughter was married and had a three-month-old baby Mary had not yet seen. Leslie lived just across the county line. She saw more of his wife than she saw him. He traveled a lot and often his job took him away from home for weeks at a time. He was a salesman for Missouri Farmers Association and covered the entire state visiting the various MFA stores and agencies. Of all of Mary's four children, Leslie, her youngest, made the most money, but it was at a personal cost of being away from his family so much. His wife, Thelma, was a wonderful mate for him, and Mary loved her dearly.

Thelma's mother and father were killed in a car accident when she was only four years old and her grandparents had raised her. Mary was "Mother" to Thelma and she called her "Mom" or "Mother" and pretended she was her real mother. Mary welcomed her love and devotion and loved more often than any of the others. Her job in the bank brought her to town every day and she often had lunch with Mary and usually called several times a week just to talk. They had no children as yet, but with her job and the chores at home she never lacked for something to do. And the long, lonely nights that Leslie was away she'd read or write letters until she was sleepy enough to go to bed. Five years married she had yet to become pregnant. She had never used any means to prevent conception and once last year had actually visited a doctor to see if maybe something was wrong with her. She was assured there was no reason she could not produce children. The doctor suggested Leslie come in for examination but her husband flat-out refused to go. Quite a quarrel had erupted that night. Later she had discussed it with Mary. Mary assured her that if for any reason Leslie could not sire children she was unaware of it. She advised Thelma to forget about it and hopefully by just relaxing and enjoying their times together it would happen. Maybe they were trying too hard. Thelma was thirty-one. She wanted babies, but she wanted a happy home too. She decided to take Mom's advice and let life take its course.

Jeanette knew her family. Their joys and sorrows were shared in a closeness many families never knew. She spent several nights with Thelma each trip back and the two women enjoyed the company of the other, bridging the difference in their ages with remarkable ease.

Mary was looking forward to a good visit with her elder daughter that night. She always spent the first night at home and skipped around the various relatives in the area later. She hadn't expected her back for supper, knowing Audrey would want her for the evening meal, but she would be back by bedtime. So engrossed was Mary in her thoughts that the shrill ringing of the telephone startled her so she nearly fell off her chair.

"Mother, I'm still at Audrey's. They want me to stay all night. Do you mind?"

"Well of course I mind. What's so important that you can't come back here to sleep?"

"We have a little project going which needs more attention at this end right now. I'll see you tomorrow and tell you all about it then. Okay?"

So that was that. Mary was so disappointed the tears slid down her cheeks. She was definitely feeling neglected. That first night had almost been sacred with closeness between mother and daughter that each looked forward to from year to year. Apparently tomorrow she would learn what the Hot Project was that couldn't wait. She took a long, leisurely tub bath and was in bed by nine o'clock. Suddenly she realized how very tired she was. She could hardly keep her eyes open while she read her nightly chapter from the Bible. Perhaps it was just as well things worked out as they did. No sooner had her head hit the pillow than Mary was asleep.

Chapter 4

Jeanette continued to stroll through the park, still stopping to speak to friends and acquaintances along the way. The excitement of the past three days still engulfed her. It was almost like being encased in a big golden bubble. Once Lee had agreed to her offer, plans had been made and carried out swiftly and efficiently.

Pedro had been loaded into the pickup Thursday morning, along with enough feed to last four days. Janie led him up the ramp with no trouble whatsoever. He was a bit nervous at finding high stock rails around him that he couldn't see over. He could see through the bars however, and with Janie beside him he actually was quite calm. Janie would ride in the back with him. At the last minute Lee handed the ignition keys to Audrey and climbed in the back, checking to make sure the in-gate was firmly in place. He felt better knowing Janie was okay.

From Wednesday evening to Saturday afternoon every minute had been filled and some of it was downright hard work. The daily crowds swelled at night and it was long after midnight before the park area quieted down enough so people could sleep. Leslie had brought Mother down to see the parade. Janie wore her long white dress Velma had made her. Jeanette had set her hair that morning and Mary was surprised, but pleased, to see her tomboy granddaughter could be a very pretty young lady when she chose to be. As FFA Queen she rode the float as regally as a real queen might have.

Mary stayed to sit through the old fiddler's contest, the band concert, and the baby contest. She rested in the camper while the others went off to the tractor pull, the chain saw contest, and the plowing contest. They even had a hog callin' in which both men and women participated. They stood in the makeshift stage and called "Suey, suey, suey, here pig, pig, pig," at the top of their lungs. Mary had no doubt but that pigs within a five-mile radius could hear them. There were several large sows in the FFA pens and all had taken blue ribbons. The lambs and ewes were groomed so clean Mary wondered if they were house pets. Of course it was all done especially for the judging but it made ordinary farm animals look very much out of place in all their finery. Pedro seemed much larger in the small pen allotted to him than he appeared at home. Having seen the puny, scrawny calf shortly after birth, Mary marveled at the wonderful job Janie had done raising him. In the beginning she would not have given two cents to his survival chances. Now look at him. He surely must weigh nearly two thousand pounds and his black coat had been brushed until it fairly glistened in the sunlight, all because of the tender loving care of one little pigtailed girl.

The doting grandmother was happy for Janie when she heard Pedro had taken a red ribbon, but she was disgusted to see blue ribbons on ugly goats and spindle-legged chickens when other beautiful creatures were not ranked as high by the judges. She knew nothing about best of breed and best of class judging.

Of all the exhibits, Mary had enjoyed the horticulture and handwork displays most. Audrey's pickled peaches and crab apples and jelly had won her some money and many of her relatives and friends picked up some extra cash in prize money for their baked goods, canned goods, rugs, quilts, fancywork, etc. They even had an art exhibit now. Mary was really surprised at the articles displayed and the artistic talent the native people possessed. She didn't know a real artist lived in the county and here was an entire tent full of pictures from approximately thirty local artists. Amateurs they may be but the work was good and Mary thought she would be proud to hang any one of the pictures in her home. She had had her share of prize money in years past but no longer contributed entries.

It was the final day of the show. Jeanette had really enjoyed the past few days and for the most part Janie had been in seventh heaven. Already, she had begun to badger Jeanette to take her vacation same time next year so they could do it all over again. Jeanette wasn't sure about that but she would think about it. She was making one final round of the various displays and exhibits and sideshows, weaving her way through the carnival grounds. The crowds were thicker here. She mused to herself that of the four adult rides she had not been on a single one. Back in her younger days she would not have passed up any of them.

Stopping to buy a bag of popcorn she happened to notice three young men standing nearby, chatting away among themselves, completely detached from the crowd, the noise around them, and the rides. She watched them for several minutes when suddenly the one leaning against a tree moved slightly and Jeanette gasped.

Chapter 5

It couldn't be of course, but my Lord, what a striking resemblance. It was like seeing a ghost. The tall, lean, handsome young man was an exact replica of someone she had known in her high school days. Someone she had known very, very well.

Her curiosity now thoroughly aroused, Jeanette knew she would have to speak to the young man if for no other reason than to learn his name. She felt she already knew but wanted to hear him say it. In the milling crowd she searched for someone nearby she knew well enough to ask them if perhaps they recognized the trio by the tree. Not a soul passing close by did she recognize. If she left to look for someone she knew to ask, the boys might be gone when she returned. It was a chance she couldn't take. She wanted to speak to him and she would speak to him. She never had been the aggressive type but neither was she shy.

Working her way through the crowd to the edge of the park where the young man was still leaning against the tall maple tree while he conversed with his friends, Jeanette halted in front of her conquest. Speaking quickly before she lost her nerve she addressed him, "Excuse me, sir. Do you know a Dan Colton?"

Three pairs of eyes now focused on her with interest. Who was she? None of them had ever seen her before. "I'm, Michael Colton. Dan Colton is my father. Do you know him?"

"Not anymore. I did know your father a long time ago."

"May I ask your name, ma'am?"

"My name isn't important. I'm just someone who knew your father many years ago."

"Please, you must tell me your name. I have told you mine. And what will I tell dad when I relate that I met an old friend of his in the park and she refused to give her name. Dad will not buy that story. He'll think I made it all up."

"I'm sorry Mr. Colton to have bothered you. I must apologize to you and your friends for intruding. Thank you for speaking with me." She turned away and would have walked into the mass of people except that Mr. Colton restrained her with his hand on her shoulder. He was loath to let her go without at least learning her name.

"Did you know my father well?"

"Well enough that he once asked me to marry him. But of course that was a long time ago, a very long time ago, and I really must go." Excusing herself once again, this time she successfully escaped into the crowd, and working her way across the throng of milling people she made her way to the camper. It was time to prepare supper.

She had been given a sackful of roasting ears from one of the FFA kids and corn on the cob would go well with the hamburgers and coleslaw and sliced tomatoes she had planned for supper. As Jeanette cleaned the corn and continued to busy herself with supper preparations her mind kept drifting back to those long ago, carefree, happy days when she was a teenager. It was as if seeing the boy had released a flood of old memories, memories that had been buried for nearly thirty years. Actually being there at the Corn Stalk Show had revived old memories and seeing the boy just opened the floodgates.

This was to be their last night. The crowds would swell to overflowing the park. The streets and sidewalks would be covered with milling, talking people. The carnival would be doing a thriving business with its rides and booths. Kids were going wild that last night. Oh how well she remembered her own escapades during that last night. The stores would be open and farmers would be doing their regular Saturday night shopping. The restaurants and theater had standing room only. In fact just about everyone in the crowd came from all over the county and outlying counties Saturday night at the Corn Stalk Show. Funny, it used to be called Corn Stalk Show. Now it was billed as Corn and Stock Show. After the final evening program, an old fiddler's contest, there was to be a street dance with five bands taking turns playing from nine to one A.M. There would be square dancing, round dancing, disco, just about every dance folks were doing nowadays. Tomorrow the excitement would be gone but the memories would remain forever. Tomorrow Lee would bring the truck and Pedro and Janie would go home and she would go back to Glenwood and have a good visit with her mother.

Chapter 6

Dan was just crawling out from under a Chevy pickup and glad to have it done. That brake job had to be finished by six P.M. His customer had said he would return at six and Dan had said it would be ready. He was proud of the garage and filling station he had worked so hard to build up. The business was good and his honesty and fairness had impressed customers so that they kept coming back and bringing or sending their friends in. Two years ago he had added a small snack bar and coffee shop, and just this summer had extended 6:00 A.M.. to 10:00 P.M. hours into twenty four-hour service. Already it was paying off.

The new highway that by-passed the town went right past his place of business now. He had highway trade as well as local business. Because of the long haul–cross-country trucks that were stopping to fill up at his place–he had decided to remain open twenty four hours a day, seven days a week, and opened up the coffee shop where coffee was always ready and breakfast was served any hour as ordered. It meant hiring four more employees but Dan felt in the long run it would pay off, and indeed it had. He now had ten people on the payroll, besides himself and his son Michael. Mike and Dan worked ten-hour shifts and took turns on night and weekends. All the employees rotated on shifts but they only worked eight hours at a time. On rare occasions when an employee worked overtime Dan was always careful to give extra pay.

The sign over the door read COLTON & SON. Dan managed the business but Mike was learning more all the time. He knew how to book the cash receipts and could order stock as well as Dan. He was a good mechanic in most engines but preferred to pump gas or diesel fuel if he had a choice, staying outside as much as possible. Even in the winter when the snowplow had to keep the lanes open in bad weather he would go out to wait on customers cheerfully.

Now Mike and his buddies gathered around Dan in some excitement. Dan looked up and recognized that something had stirred the boys up, and from all appearances he was to be let in on it immediately.

Mike spoke first. "All right old man. You've been holding out on me. I've often wondered about your love life in your younger days but never asked questions. Figured that was your business and you were entitled to your privacy. You told me my mother ran off with a man she met in a bar when I was two months old and that's why we lived with Aunt Faye. I accepted all that you told me. We moved into the apartment in town, just you and me when I was thirteen. And we've learned to adjust.

"We just met a lady in that park, Mark, Tom, and I, and she was asking about you. She seemed quite interested in me, but somehow I don't think this woman is my mother. But, damn it, dad, I've got to know for sure. You never spoke about her except just to say she left you when I was a tiny baby. Aunt Faye said you even destroyed every picture of her you had, including some that she had of the two of you together. She said you had no right to tear them out of her album but you were hurt at the time, that she didn't make an issue of it. Besides, with three girls she and Uncle Carl were tickled to have a little boy around the house. And she insisted you live there too so they could look after you as well."

Finally Mike had to stop for breath and Dan quickly jumped in before Mike could continue. "Will you please stop rattling on and tell me exactly what it is you're trying to say?"

"My mother. Is that woman in the park my mother? You always said you never knew where she was or even if she was alive. Now I wonder! Maybe you did know all along and never told me."

"For Pete's sakes, Mike. What's with you? I know you missed not having a mother but I never knew it affected you all that much. Faye loved you and cared for you as much as any real mother could, which is a heap more than your own mother did. And as God is my witness, I have never seen or heard from her since the day she left. And that is the truth. Now, about this woman you met in the park. How did you meet her?"

"She walked right up to us and very politely requested permission to speak to us. And then she asked me if I was related to a Dan Colton. When I told her I was your son she nodded, as if she thought as much all along. She apologized for being so forward and asking questions and then thanked me, thanked us all in fact, for taking up our time, and left us."

"Well, what was her name? She surely introduced herself?"

"That she didn't. In fact she wouldn't tell us even when I asked for her name. Just said she was someone you knew a long time ago and her name didn't matter. Then she walked away."

All during the entire conversation Mark and Tom had stood silently by, taking in everything being said without making any comment themselves. This was all very interesting to them and they were most intrigued by the entire episode and desired to learn more about the strange lady and her connection to Dan Colton. They had known Mike and his dad all their lives and never knew Dan to womanize. He never showed any interest in the female sex and often was polite with effort when one tried to get too personal. He refused to become involved either sexually or emotionally. Some thought him bitter because of his wife having left him but he had a good repartee with women customers who were regulars at the station. True, most of his women customers were happily married, but there were a few who were not. One divorcee in particular had tested him out, offering more than just a casual friendliness, however, he had politely turned her down. She was still a customer but now no longer made advances toward a romance between them.

Not wanting to appear too interested and yet not willing to let the subject drop, Dan casually questioned the young man.

"What did this lady look like? Was she tall, short, fat, slim?" Surely there was something about her that stood out in the memory of their short and rather brief encounter.

Mike spoke first in answer to his father's questions. "The thing that keeps running in my mind is when I asked her if she knew you well, she replied that she once knew you so well that at one time you had asked her to marry you, but it had happened a long time ago. She was very pretty and actually blushed when she apologized for her sudden intrusion and just as suddenly disappeared in the crowd."

Mark told Dan the lady was tall and slender and wore the blue white pantsuit with the ease and grace of a true lady. She had red hair with just a touch of gray at the temple. Her hair formed a soft halo around her face, a very becoming style, and it looked natural red, not dyed or hennaed at all.

It was Tom's comments Dan was most pleased with for after Mark's description he knew who their mysterious lady was. There was only one redhead he had ever wanted to marry and she turned him down and later married someone else. He used to see her in later years occasionally around the community, usually with two small boys in town. Then he had heard she had left the county with her husband and small children and gone out of state where her husband had a new job. It had been twenty-five years since he had last seen or heard of her. But even after all these years he never had completely got her out of his system.

Now Tom was saying, "We know where she's staying, Dan. I doubt that she knew we were following her as we kept our distance and still kept her in sight. She entered a blue camper parked near the bull arena, so she must be connected in some way with the young people in the FFA Program.

There are some good looking calves there in various pens, and goats and sheep and the funniest looking chickens you ever saw."

The boys immediately glimpsed the light of recognition in Dan's eyes.

"Are you going to see her, Dad?"

"Do you want me to get shot? I doubt if her husband would approve of an unexpected visit to his wife from one of her old flames."

"Did you really ask her to marry you?"

"Yes, and she turned me down. That all happened long before I met your mother."

"Well, I still think you should go see her, just for old times' sake. Surely her husband would have no objection to a conversation held in the open."

"Well, I don't know. I'm about ready to leave here. Who's on tonight?"

Chapter 7

Dan showered, put on his new slacks and pullover shirt. It wouldn't hurt to walk around the grounds–quite a crowd over there tonight. The midway was a blaze of lights and the music was so loud it could be heard for blocks away. Maybe, just maybe he could catch a glimpse of her.

Arriving at the far end of the park where the bandstand was and where the seats were set up, he scanned the lines of benches where people were resting and visiting among themselves.

Moving on he stopped briefly by the ferris wheel, looking closely at the mass of people. Where did they all come from? A few people spoke to him in passing. This was his town but it certainly overflowed with strangers when the carnival came to town. There were seven rides in all and all were doing great, business-wise. Every ride was full and probably would remain for the rest of the evening. The side shows and game booths had people standing in line. In his younger days he had always enjoyed a good carnival, with the ferris wheel being his favorite ride. He never attended carnivals anymore and it had been ten to fifteen years since he had ridden the ferris wheel. As his mind wandered back, memories flooded in. Now he was remembering the good times, the happy times. Moving leisurely through the crowd he slowly progressed toward the stock pens. The lights weren't as bright here and the odor of cattle was strong in the air. Although quite a number of people were milling around, still there was not the density of the midway. From all appearances the stock had been bedded down for the night. The pens had clean straw strewn about and the water was clear and up to the full mark in the drinking pails.

Really some good looking animals here, all of which looked like prize winners to him. He wondered which ones belonged to his friend.

There were twenty campers or thereabouts scattered around the living quarters area, with a few tents set up here and there. Hard to guess which belonged to the carnival crew and which were FFA representatives. Not far from the stall where a huge Black Angus was penned he spotted the blue camper on a blue Chevy pickup with Arizona license plates. The camper door was open and all inside lights were on. Three young teenage girls seemed to be moving about inside.

He leaned against the lamppost mustering up enough courage to go to the door and knock. Suddenly the young people spilled out, followed by a woman. The woman shut and locked the camper door. The girls took off for the midway without a backward glance. His heart skipped a beat as he watched the woman. God, the years had been good to her. He hadn't seen her in over twenty years and yet she was the same slim, pretty girl he had loved so long ago. He knew he couldn't let her pass without speaking to her.

Jeanette thought she would play some bingo while watching for Audrey and Lee to show up. They were always late arriving because all chores had to be completed before Lee would leave the farm. It had been a hectic weekend, but Jeanette was glad she had a part in the annual celebration. It had meant so much to her niece and she herself had enjoyed the past three days. It was certainly a change from her usual vacation.

Moving away from the living quarters Jeanette suddenly tripped over a tent guy wire. She would have fallen full length upon the hard ground had she not been caught up in strong arms as she toppled downwards. She was held a few seconds before her rescuer set her upright.

"Are you all right? You very nearly had a nasty spill there."

"Yes, I think so. I didn't see that wire in the dim light. I should have been watching where I was going." Her leg was stinging and she looked down to see if her pant leg was torn.

"Are you sure you are not hurt? That wire must have given you quite a sting."

For the first time Jeanette looked into the face of her rescuer, and she gasped as instant recognition set in. "Dan! Dan! Is it really you? Was it fate that brought you to my rescue?"

"I don't know about fate, but I'm glad to be of service. And it wasn't accidental that I happened to be here tonight. When my son and his friends spoke of your encounter this evening I knew it had to be you. I wanted to speak to you. You haven't changed much."

Jeanette's leg was really hurting now and she felt she should examine it more closely. "Dan, come into the camper with me. I'll make some coffee and we'll talk and catch up on family happenings during the past years."

It was an invitation Dan would not turn down.

Upon entering the camper Dan first noticed the female clothing strewn over the bunk beds. Girls' domain. Nothing to the naked eye showed that a man lived on the premises.

Jeanette put fresh water and coffee in the percolator and sat it on the burner. Then sitting down in the booth she pulled her pant leg up to reveal an ugly, red welt just above the ankle. Dan saw it also and grimaced. "Sorry I couldn't prevent that."

"Is that fresh coffee I smell?" Lee stuck his head in the door and stepped inside before noticing Dan sitting at the table. "Sorry Sis, I didn't know you had company."

"Sit down and have some coffee." The introductions were made and her near accident explained as well as Dan's rescuing her from a bad fall. Feeling a bit shaken and wanting to examine any damage done, Jeanette told Lee she had returned to the camper and invited Dan to join her. Dan was an old friend from her high school days and she hadn't seen or heard of him in twenty-five years or so, and common courtesy was to invite him in for a cup of coffee. And where were Audrey and the girls.

"Slow down, Sis. I'm not berating or criticizing you for discovering a man in your camper, just surprised is all. Velma and her boyfriend are somewhere on the grounds and Audrey had to ride the ferris wheel with Ree. I came by to check on Pedro. Suppose Janie has already taken off for the bright light?"

"Yes, she and two of her girlfriends left only a few minutes ago. She took care of Pedro right after supper. Oh, Lee, you've got so much to be proud of in that girl. She's done wonders with that calf. And she is as proud of that red ribbon as if it was one hundred dollars. And you should have seen her this afternoon, so pretty in her long white dress with her long hair curling loose-ly about her face. She was FFA Queen, you know. It was such a disappoint-ment to her that her mother wasn't watching the parade. She thinks she's the only FFA participant who did not have at least one parent attending."

"Wow! Unlike you to hit below the belt."

"Well, it's your own fault. You can't be insensitive to the needs and wants of a sensitive little girl without a breach growing between the two of you."

Jeanette poured three cups of coffee and cut two slices of pie. She had baked two pies that morning and the girls had devoured one at supper. Fresh apple pie was one of Lee's favorites.

"Mind if I come in? That coffee smells mighty good." Audrey entered the camper and made Lee scoot over so she could sit down beside him. Jeanette poured another cup of coffee and put it in front of her sister.

"Want some pie?"

"Sure!" She cut another slice and set it on a saucer and reaching into the drawer for another fork, handed the saucer to Audrey.

"How come you're not eating pie?"

"Because I've already had two pieces today and that is quite enough. Audrey, you remember Dan Colton?"

"I thought that's who it was, but I wasn't sure. It's been a long time. Nice to see you again Dan."

Audrey was told about Jeanette's accident and how Dan had suddenly appeared out of nowhere to break her fall. She showed her leg to Audrey where the wire had left its mark. Now that she was on safe ground and with Lee and Audrey sitting there she turned her attention to the man she now sat beside.

"Your son is a fine looking young man. Looks like you. Do you and your family live around here? I remember Queen City used to be your old stomping grounds."

"Yes, Mike and I live here in an apartment over the drugstore. My wife left me when Mike was just a baby. I haven't seen her since. Of course I got a divorce right away and custody of Mike. We lived with my sister until Mike was nearly grown. We've been in the apartment ever since. I own a garage and service station here in town and until Mike wishes to do otherwise he works with me. The sign over the door says 'Colton and Son.' Mike has taken to the business like a natural and I hope someday he'll really take over and I can retire. He's never known anything else and doesn't seem to be interested in any other way of life. I had set money aside all through the years that he might have a college education. You know, I never finished high school, myself. But Mike didn't have any desire to go to college. He did finish high school for which I'm glad. He wants to stay on at the station. Of course that's no disgrace. We have an honest, reliable business, but it is a bit depressing to me that he has so little ambition."

"I know how you feel. We have three daughters, two of them teenagers. Audrey and I have saved and scrimped through the years, banking the profits from the cattle so the girls could attend college. And wouldn't you know it, they aren't interested. One wants to get married and one wants to farm."

Dan felt at ease with these nice people. "And your family Jeanette! Your children are grown and married I suppose! Is your husband here with you?"

"My husband is deceased. The boys–I have two sons–are married, and I have three grandchildren. I still maintain my home in Arizona and am still working. I suppose I could retire, but I like working. Right now I'm on thirty-day leave."

"I'm sorry to hear about your husband's passing. Were your children very young when he died?" And Dan truly felt compassion in his heart for his old friend.

"I've been a widow for more than two years now, almost three. Ed was sick a long time before he died. He was able to enjoy his grandchildren before the illness became too intense. Little Pete was such a blessing to him. Petey was only two when his grandfather passed away. They were so close. We had feared it would be a difficult time for him but the little fellow seemed to understand that Grandpa no longer was suffering. We explained that heaven was a place where there was no more hurt. Petey had seen him when he was very low on various occasions and he missed him but wanted

Grandpa to stay in that place all the time where there was no more pain. Petey didn't quite understand about heaven but he did know about pain."

Audrey got up and picked up the empty pie saucers and rinsing them off, set them in the sink. "More coffee anyone?"

"Jeanette, where is your medical kit? I know you always carry one. You'd best dab something on that leg. With all the dust and germs around here infection could quite easily set in."

"Oh, I don't think so. The skin wasn't broken." She got up and opened a cabinet door and took down the tin box marked Red Cross Medical Kit. She hadn't opened it in months so couldn't remember exactly just what was in it. Was it last spring Larry had used some Band-Aids from the box?

Audrey took the box from her, opened it and extracted a small bottle of iodine. "Iodine isn't what I would normally use on a welt, nevertheless the cream ointment will not kill infection as effectively, so sit down again and lets have another look at that leg."

Jeanette obeyed without further argument or comment and leaned back against Dan's shoulder to give Audrey more room to daub away with the iodine. She hardly realized what she had done, yet for some reason she felt a warm glow slip over her at contact. Good Lord! Wishing to put distance between them before Audrey or Lee could jump to conclusions, wrong conclusions, Jeanette suggested they return to the midway. It was Audrey who invited Dan to join them. He quite willingly accepted because he had no intention of letting Jeanette disappear from his life once again. His mind was already busy working out a strategy to see her again and as often as possible while she was here. Now he was older and wiser and more determined. He would move slow, win her confidence and trust, and when she was ready, would teach her to love him. His confidence was sure, but of course none of this did he let on to the others.

Passing the tent where she had tripped over the offensive wire she pointed it out to the others and very carefully they all stepped around it.

"Someone should tie white strips of cloth along that guy," Lee surmised aloud. Although it was lit up enough to see to get by, the sleeping quarters were only dimly lighted. A wire that close to the ground could easily be overlooked, especially if one wasn't paying too close attention to where they were going. Lee's hand moved to take Audrey's elbow, an unconscious effort to guide her to safer ground. Lee could be mean at times but he was always protective and gentle with Audrey. They had married while still in high school and he had never wanted another woman. Even his disappointment in having no sons would in no way put the blame on his wife. It was just one of those things.

Passing the food stand, Audrey remarked it was a good thing they had already eaten, as people were standing in long lines waiting to sit down and be served. The stand-up quick counter was double lined and the smell of frying hamburgers and hot dogs was pungent. The flies were so bad that

Jeanette herself never liked to eat at the stands. Couldn't be helped of course out in the open like that. She knew that at night when the park was closed that the Jaycees sprayed all the grounds, doing what they could to control the population of flies. Funny, there were more flies here than around the stock pens.

Seeing five people leave the bingo stand, Audrey immediately sat down and motioned the others to fill the gap. Dan and Lee exchanged amused glances. Looked like they were about to play whether they had a mind to or not. Sooner or later Audrey could always be found at the bingo stand. All the family knew this and it was here that Ree spotted her mother and came trotting over, squeezing in on the board seat between her mother and her aunt. Most adults played two or three cards at a time. Audrey playing two and she silently slipped one over in front of Ree. Ree could manage one card very well by herself but her mother always kept a watchful eye on any card she played anyway. This would have disgusted the little girl had she known.

After five games and none of them winning they all moved in mutual accord away from the counter making room for others just waiting to get in.

"Will you buy me some cotton candy, Aunt Jeanette?"

"Now sis, you very well know you have your own spending money for tonight. Don't be begging from your Aunt Jeanette." Lee chided Ree, surprised that she would even ask.

"It's all right Lee. I don't mind. And besides, I wouldn't mind having some myself." Taking Ree by the hand she led the way across the small space to a stand where hot popcorn, peanuts, candied apples, *and* the requested candy cotton was sold. She put in their order and reached inside her light jacket pocket for the money to pay for it. She carried only a few dollars on her and kept her purse locked in the cabinet drawer over her bed. The bed pillows hid the drawer and she felt that should her camper be broken into, unless it was a professional doing a thorough search, her purse would not be spotted. She had never had a break-in, but still she took precautions.

"Ninety cents, please!"

"My treat!" And before Jeanette could count out the change, Dan had already paid for the spun candy and bought a box of popcorn as well.

"Who are you?" Ree never was real bashful but she knew she shouldn't let strangers buy her candy, and she instinctively backed against her aunt, taking hold of her free hand, afraid to let go as she looked up at the tall man smiling down at her. Dan was amused and yet charmed by this precocious child. Here might well be an ally in his campaign.

"Ree, this is Mr. Colton, a very old friend of mine. Dan, my niece, Ree, Audrey and Lee's youngest." They each acknowledged the brief introduction and Ree said aloud that is was all right then, if Mr. Colton was a friend of her Aunt Jeanette. And she thanked him for her sweet.

"Yes, please accept my thanks also!"

"My pleasure! And now could I interest you in riding the ferris wheel? It has been years since I've ridden. With two lovely ladies beside me I could ride all night."

Oh yes, Aunt Jeanette, let's do!" It didn't matter that she had just gotten off a short time before, she never tired of the big wheel. Most rides were too short anyway.

Looking back to where they had left Audrey and Lee, Jeanette caught her sister's eye and motioned toward the ferris wheel. She still held Ree's hand, and as casually as if it was an everyday occurrence, Dan led the girls to the ticket booth where he bought quite a string of tickets. As his eyes met Jeanette's he grinned impudently and pocketed all but three tickets. It wasn't long until they were seated, Ree in the middle.

Chapter 8

It was nine A.M. Jeanette and Janie had been up for two hours. They had breakfasted and packed up what needed to be packed up for moving on. Pedro had been fed and watered and his stall cleaned. Lee should be arriving any minute with the truck.

Jeanette could not get last night out of her mind. They had ridden the ferris wheel for almost an hour, much to Ree's great pleasure. Lee and Audrey had stopped by and watched and waited but Ree didn't want to get off until all the tickets were used up and so it was. They talked about past rides and Dan cautiously slipped his arm across the back of the seat and across her shoulders. She hadn't commented and it remained there for some time. She was remembering other times and other rides when he had rocked the chair when they were stopped on the very top, frightening her a bit, teasing her. He had taken her in his arms and kissed her and she had been furious with him. Did he remember?

The final drawings were held at ten-thirty P.M. after which the crowd immediately began to thin out. They had all returned to the camper for more coffee, with Ree eating the last piece of pie. Velma and her boyfriend had stopped off briefly. Velma preferred the camper's toilet to the public rest rooms in the park. She was told by Lee to be home by midnight and her young man assured him he would have her home before midnight.

Dan asked Jeanette if he might see her again, perhaps to take her to dinner the next day. She declined the dinner invitation because she felt her mother would be expecting her, but agreed to dine with him at a later date. He knew where her mother lived and would call her later in the week.

Now it was morning. Lee was backing in. He was alone. Audrey and the girls had taken the car and gone into Livonia to Sunday school and church. Most of the FFA stock had already been removed and the temporary pens were being disassembled and loaded for return to the county fairgrounds from which they had been borrowed. The carnival was in disarray with booths dismantled and rides being pulled apart and loaded onto the big trucks. Next stop for the carnival was two hundred miles down the road and it had to open on Wednesday.

Pedro was acting nervous. He didn't want to board the trailer. No amount of coaxing from Janie would entice him to walk up the ramp and through the trailer gate. Lee was beginning to lose patience when Dan Colton walked in on the scene.

"Good morning. Looks like you could use some help here." He spoke directly to Lee and merely nodded his head toward Jeanette and Janie.

"Good morning Mr. Colton. Pedro is being stubborn. He never acted up like this at home." Janie saw her dad was losing his patience.

"What can I do to help? I've never been around farm animals much but I'll do what I can."

Janie moved up into the trailer, softly calling the big animal by name. "Get back daddy. All of you stand away." She began speaking softly, coaxingly, "Come on Pedro, come on now boy" As if mesmerized Pedro lumbered up the ramp and permitted the slip of a girl to pat his nose and stroke his forehead.

"Good boy! Good boy Pedro! Now we're going home." Lee slammed the tailgate shut and Janie climbed out over the side. Soon they would be home, but the past four days would linger in Janie's mind for a long, long time to come.

After good-byes were said and Lee and Janie had both profusely thanked Jeanette for her part in the past few days, the pickup began to weave its way off the carnival grounds and into the street. It was only a short distance to the open highway.

"Have you had breakfast?"

"No! Have you?"

"Sorta! Janie was so excited we only had rolls and hot chocolate. I'll make some coffee but I've already packed everything down tight for moving out. I'm going straight to Mom's from here."

"Please have breakfast with me. The restaurant across the street isn't open on Sunday but my place of business is open twenty–four hours a day. Go with me and I'll treat you to the finest breakfast you've ever eaten."

"You make it hard to say no."

"Then don't say no. Say yes. Come on."

Jeanette knew her mother would be in Sunday school and church for the next two hours. It was less than half an hour's drive to her mother's house. She knew her mother would not expect her before noon.

"All right, your kind invitation is accepted. Now if you aren't afraid to ride with a woman driver we'll be off to this eating palace. But afterwards I really must go. Okay?"

"Okay!"

They walked toward her truck. Jeanette went inside the camper and got her purse. She then locked up the camper and unlocked the cab door. Dan held the door open while she climbed in behind the wheel. She leaned over and unlocked the passenger door as he walked around the truck. She had run the motor a little each day so it wouldn't be hard to start. Now it came to life immediately, for which she was thankful. Carefully backing out of her place she skillfully wove in and out among various objects, people, moving vehicles, and even a group of goats that had somehow gotten loose. Reaching the street she turned to her companion and said, "Which way?"

The small diner had seating for perhaps twenty-five or thirty people. There were four booths, two small tables with chairs, and eight stools at the counter. Two men, possibly occupants of the semi being serviced outside sat at the counter. They had just been served steak, eggs, hash browns, and toast on a platter. Lordy, if each man got around that plateful he wouldn't need to eat for the rest of the day. Both men greeted Dan cordially and asked how it was going. Jeanette didn't care for the way they looked her over. Dan introduced her to the men and to the waitress/cook, explaining she was an old friend whom he hadn't seen for many years, who had only recently returned to town.

"Two more orders of steak and eggs, Rhoda." Leading Jeanette to the corner table he gallantly pulled a chair out and seated her. Then going behind the counter he poured two cups of coffee and carried them back to the table. He even remembered from the night before that she drank her coffee hot and black.

"You must change my order. I couldn't possibly eat all that," and she nodded toward the counter where the truck drivers were doing swift justice to what was on their plates.

"Sure you can eat it. I promised you a good breakfast and that's what you're getting. In fact you aren't leaving here until you eat every bite."

"Dan, please! Had I known you were going to be difficult I wouldn't have come. In fact I've a good notion to leave right now."

"Not before you eat, my girl! Not before you eat!"

"Are you serious?"

"Quite!"

The two drivers looked at each other and grinned. They had listened to the conversation and each had wondered if old Dan had at last gotten himself a woman. Finishing their meal they were washing it down with another coffee when the station attendant came in and informed them the rig was ready to go. One man went outside to move the truck out of the drive and the other man followed the attendant into the station to settle his bill.

"Um! It looks and smells delicious. Rhoda, you are one fine cook. Dig in honey, while it's still hot."

Despite all her talk of not being hungry Jeanette discovered she was in fact very hungry. She saw Dan had cut a small piece of his steak, using only his fork. She did likewise. Once beginning to eat it seemed she couldn't stop. Glancing up she met the eyes head-on of the man sitting across from her and he was grinning from ear to ear.

"Well, don't stop now. You're doing fine. Good, isn't it?"

"Every bite is just delicious. And the coffee is good, too. The meat you buy in Arizona is a far cry from this." She pushed her plate aside and picked up her coffee cup, slowly sipping the hot liquid.

The outside door opened and the two truckers came back in. They each carried a thermos. "Rhoda, baby! How about filling these up and we'll be on our way?"

Rhoda took both bottles and emptied the contents out and thoroughly rinsed them before refilling with freshly made coffee.

"You know gal, you're the only one on the entire circuit who does that. We appreciate it." They paid for their meal, coffee, bought more cigarettes and chewing gum, and left. Jeanette noticed each had left the waitress a dollar tip.

"Quit stalling unless you want to stay all day, which won't make me a bit unhappy. You still have one egg, half your spuds and half that steak to go."

"You really are kidding?"

"Nope!" And to emphasize his point he pushed the plate back in front of her. She picked up her fork and put another bite of steak in her mouth. Oh how good it was. She would at least eat all the meat. With today's prices it would be a shame to have it thrown out.

Several customers came in. They spoke or nodded to Dan and he spoke and nodded back. Rhoda came over and reheated their coffee. Dan asked for some more jelly, which she promptly brought. Jeanette had eaten only one slice of toast and she now slid the other two slices on Dan's plate of toast.

"No you don't, Mi-lady. *You* eat that *and* the rest of your eggs."

"I can't. I really can't. Normally I have juice, toast, and coffee. Sometimes I'll scramble a couple eggs for supper. Often I take off for work after just a quick cup of instant coffee."

"Well that certainly isn't smart. And I suppose you skip lunch as well."

"Sometimes. Quite often in fact."

"You need a keeper, woman. Even animals know enough to eat. No wonder you've stayed so slim all these years. You look great but a few more pounds won't do you no harm."

"Are you criticizing me, Dan Colton?"

"Only your eating habits, luv," and he smiled that tantalizing smile that always had left her weak in the past. It was no different now. Why had he popped back into her life after all these years? With her thoughts on the past she unconsciously took another bite of toast and put another fork full of eggs in her mouth. He sat silently sipping his coffee, watching her as she continued to eat, deep in her own thoughts, almost as if she had forgotten he was there. Finally he noted her plate was empty and she even ate the last piece of toast. He broke in on her musings.

"See! I told you you could do it," indicating the empty platter.

"Oh! Good gosh! I didn't eat all that?"

"Yep! You sure did. Took you awhile though. Where were you just now? You seemed to be far away in a world all your own."

"Sorry! I'm afraid I was far away. About thirty-four years away. I was eighteen."

He watched the red flush that appeared in her cheeks as she looked up at him. Surely a woman in her fifties didn't blush. Even the young girls no longer blushed or so he had been told. Leaning over the small table he suddenly kissed her lightly on the cheek.

"Please don't!"

"I couldn't help myself. I'm not going to apologize. It came to me that your blush was so natural, so enchanting, I had to kiss you. Was I in your musings back there?"

Unable to speak at the moment Jeanette nodded her head affirmative.

"I'm glad. I'm very glad. Tell me, Jeanette, what was the real reason you turned me down? I never did accept that bit about being too young and wanting a career. I wouldn't have stopped you from a career. You know I wouldn't as long as you were mine. And don't say you didn't care, for I know you did. I thought my life was shattered when we busted up."

"Well, you couldn't have been too broken up. You married soon afterwards as I remember. Only a few weeks later. School wasn't out even."

"That upset you, did it?"

"More than I ever told anyone. I cried after reading your nuptials in the paper. When graduation was over I left the very next day for college where I concentrated heavily on my studies. It was the first time I had been out of state on my own. It was all new. So much to take in. I kept extremely busy and went home only on holidays. To go just for a weekend was too expensive, and beside I had a part-time job and worked after school and on weekends."

"You still haven't answered my question. Why did you turn me down? And I want the absolute truth."

Biting her lip as if loath to answer she hesitated a few seconds before speaking. "Do you remember Uncle Cal?"

"The lush who lived in your mother's upstairs apartment?" Seeing her nod he went on to say he never would forget the time he had just stepped inside the front door when all hell broke loose. A man decidedly drunk was beating a woman about the face with his fists and before anyone could intervene he had literally knocked her down the stairs where she lay whimpering in a crumpled heap. Your mother got between them and somehow got him back upstairs. You whisked me out the door real fast. As I remember, you weren't scared at all. You were mad clear through. I believe you said that if a man ever treated you like that you'd kill him."

Again she nodded. "I still feel the same way. In all the years I knew my husband he never took a drink to my knowledge, not one. He was a teeto-taler and had no patience with those who did–even beer drinkers. We never attended the parties of our friends when we knew the liquor would be flowing freely.

"You're stalling Jeanette. You still haven't given me a straight answer to my question," and he gave her a stern look as if to say his patience was running out.

"Because of my uncle I saw firsthand what alcohol could do to a man. Uncle Cal and Aunt Vena had great love and respect for each other. They were a very devoted couple with eyes only for each other. Proud, too. It was that pride that stopped them asking for help. Cal was such a good husband and father, good provider too, when he wasn't drinking. He never could hold his liquor. After a few drinks he always got mean, nasty mean. Once he got in a fight in a tavern and someone knifed him. He nearly bled to death before the sheriff and doctor got him to the hospital. Doc put eighteen stitches in his side and stomach. He spent two weeks in the hospital. Had he not been a self-employed truck driver he probably would have lost his job. There were no charges filed because both men were drunk at the time. One window, some chairs, a table, and a mirror were broken during the fight and the sheriff saw to it that Uncle Cal and his opponent paid the barkeep for damages done. With no money coming in, they got behind in their rent three months.

"When he could work again the hospital had to be paid off first. Mom depended on rent money to support us along with her meager earnings, but somehow we got by. We always raised big gardens and canned a lot to carry us through the winter. We ate rabbit for meat and chicken on Sunday. There was enough for all. It was six months before Cal got drunk again.

"Once again he came home late at night from a long haul. He had unloaded and collected his pay and stopped at a bar on the way home. He had been away ten days. Arriving home he tried to make love to Aunt Vena. Only this time he was so obnoxious and stinking she wasn't having any. He was mean drunk and not in his right mind. He was cussing her and hitting her with his fists when Jon, their eleven-year old-son entered the room. He told his dad to get away from his mother or he'd kill him. And sure enough, he had a loaded rifle pointed right at his father. Cal made a lunge for the boy and Jon pulled the trigger. The bullet hit Cal in the shoulder. Now the entire household was up. Mom, being a nurse patched him up as best she could but she couldn't take the bullet out. By now, Uncle Cal had passed out cold across the foot of the bed from booze and exhaustion not to mention his wound. We kids all went back to bed and Mom and Aunt Vena undressed and bathed Uncle Cal and got him into bed. Next day Doc came and took the bullet out. Of course a bullet wound would have to be registered with the sheriff.

"The sheriff had known Cal all his life and was quite aware of the situation as it existed. Now he put it to him real straight. Someone was going to get killed eventually if this business didn't stop. It wouldn't do any good to throw him in jail because as soon as he sobered up he'd have to turn him loose. Vena refused to press charges.

"The sheriff got a court order to send Uncle Cal to an alcoholic institution for drying out. He agreed to go. He got in the car with the sheriff and young Jon was screaming, "I hate you, I hate you, I hate you. I never want to see you again." Tears were running down Cal's cheeks when they drove off.

"Because Jon threatened to run away if his dad returned home, Aunt Vena packed up and left on the noon bus. We surmised she went home to her people. However, when Cal did return home he went at once to his in-laws and learned they never had been there and didn't even know they were missing. She must have known that was the first place he'd look for them and never let her parents know she had split. Uncle Cal took it real hard. He always blamed himself, but he never went back to drinking. And he constantly searched for his family. Vena's father passed away later that year and they couldn't notify her of his death because no one knew where she was. On Yes! A lot of things happened that year I graduated from high school. Some things will linger in my mind the rest of my life."

"Honey, I swear I'm going to shake you if you don't tell me why you refused to marry me."

"I'm coming to that. Because of Uncle Cal I swore I would never marry a beer drinking man. And *you* were a beer drinking man."

"My God! How did you know that? I always thought you never knew. Certainly I never drank in your presence. I loved you and respected you too much to let you see me like that."

'Well, I knew."

"How did you find out?"

"You broke too many dates. You missed work on too many *sick* days when I knew you had never had a sick day in your life. Once my brother saw you in a Kirksville honky-tonk. You were with a group of men and all of you, to the last man, were very much soused. Later, Wilbur told me. That night you hadn't even bothered to call and cancel the date. I got ready to go out and you never showed. Yet on our next meeting you asked me to marry you. I could never go through what Aunt Vena endured nor would I put my children through a life like that. I was crazy about you at that time but I was young, barely eighteen, and goodness knows how I could manage but I had to get you out of my system. Going to college out of state helped. I kept so busy there was no time to pine."

"God in Heaven, girl! Why didn't you tell me this at the time? Surely you never thought I would treat you like that?"

40

"When a man is drunk he has no control over his actions. Uncle Cal was always remorseful afterwards and especially sweet to Aunt Vena–until the next time. Always there was a next time."

"When Mike was a baby I stopped drinking. Quit cold! My brother-in-law spent hundreds of dollars those first two years bailing me out of Kirksville jail on drunken driving charges. I couldn't seem to get my act together. I could forget only when tanked up. Sis wouldn't let me near the baby. My own kid. Finally my driver's license was revoked for one year. Sis said one more spree and they would go to court, have me declared an unfit parent and petition for custody of my son. I would be kicked out in the street *and* no visitation rights. I had a lawyer friend check into it and learned it was possible she could do just that. That really shook me up.

"I met Mike's mother in a bar in Kirksville and we were both drunk when we got married. Got licensed and hitched by Justice of the Peace. Why he married us in the shape we were in haunts me to this day. But he did and that's water over the dam now. All she wanted was a meal ticket. Guess there never was any real love between us. Mostly I was disgusted. When she learned she was pregnant she went wild. Called me every name in the book. She said she'd kill herself if I didn't help her get rid of the baby. Abortions were almost unheard of then. One doctor flatly refused and would not give us any references as to who could or would. No one in our circle had ever had it done or even knew who to contact.

"Liz was a bitch all during her pregnancy, but she did finally have the baby. A healthy boy. Most of his care fell on me. Me, who knew nothing about babies! But I learned to bathe, feed, and change him. Even prepared formula. Liz never professed any love for him and wouldn't touch him whenever anyone else was around. My whole life was tied up in that little tyke. God, how I loved him. Liz took to going out at night while I stayed home and babysat. More often than not I fixed my own meals and cleaned the house as well. I suspicioned she was sleeping around and one day she was gone and never came back. Michael was only two months old at the time.

"That was when we moved out of the apartment and in with Sis and her family. That was when I really started hitting the bottle. Liz was good riddance. I went to the judge, told my story when I was cold sober, got a court document stating I was legal father of Michael and had sole custody, so Liz couldn't come in at a later date and try to claim him and take him away. At that same time I applied for a divorce on grounds of desertion. Because she had left a helpless infant as well as me, the proceedings were speeded up and in no time at all I was a free man, no longer married. Those two documents I keep safely locked up in my safety deposit box at the bank.

"When I quit drinking, I quit for good. Those two years were a living hell and I am thankful that Mike was too young to remember them. Of course I could never have done it without the support of my sister and her family. Once in a blue moon I'd have a beer with the guys, never over two or three in an evening, and I've never been drunk since. And that is the God Almighty truth."

"I'm surprised you never remarried. All these years and a child to care for."

"I swore off women when I swore off drinking. You might say I was a two-time loser and I wasn't interested in a third chance. Had I known your true feelings back then you would never have gotten away, you know. My son and your sons could have been *our* sons."

"Good Lord, it's almost noon. I must be going. Thanks for breakfast. It's been nice seeing you again."

Dan walked to the truck with her, saying he would call her tomorrow.

Chapter 9

Never had nights and days gone so fast. Now it was time to pack up and head back out west. For the first time in many years Jeanette really wasn't ready to go. Her mother didn't want her to go. They had such a nice visit and Mary felt such a close kinship to her oldest daughter. She would miss her terribly. She tried in vain to convince her to take her retirement and return to spend her days living with her. Mary knew she would not have many good years left. She lived in that big old house alone. What would happen to her when she could no longer care for herself? She could always go into a nursing home but somehow she hoped she'd die before that came to pass. Also she had the apartment rented to lovely folks who had been with her for nine years now, but it wasn't their responsibility to look after her. Already they had taken over the yard work and she had let them have the large garden area for several years now. She kept only a small plot for her own use where she planted a few tomato plants, some lettuce and radishes, green onions, and always her prize zinnias from which she saved the seed year after year.

Dan didn't want her to go either. On each of their dates the tension built higher, his love and need stronger. He tried to move slowly. He wanted to do it right this time. He had seen her or at least talked to her on the phone every day. He came alive in her presence and even endured a lot of teasing from Mike and the gang at work, good naturedly. Last night he had eaten supper with Jeanette and her mother. Afterwards they had ridden out into the country and he had parked the car in one of their old favorite haunts. It was her last night. Tomorrow she would be leaving for her home and job and he didn't see how he could let her go. He remembered taking her here in bygone days and how she would turn in her seat and allow him to hold her in his arms, kissing and caressing her until he was on fire with desire.

She had responded then with an equal passion but always stopped him when he wanted to go beyond mere kisses. Lordy, the cold showers he had taken because of this woman.

Now as he looked at her in the pale moonlight he saw how stiff and rigid she sat in her seat. She was looking straight ahead, off to the side, in every direction, anywhere, everywhere, but at him.

"Something wrong, honey?"

She could not speak but shook her head indicating no. Now she looked at him. With one finger he gently tilted her chin upwards so that their eyes met. She produced a feeble grin. He was so tuned in to her that he sensed she was on the verge of tears, and he was puzzled, wondering why. It had been a wonderful evening. He thought all had gone well. Mary was a gracious hostess, the best of cooks, and he liked her. She had always been decent with him even years ago when he first courted Jeanette. She was equally courteous and friendly now.

They all had laughed and kidded around and after supper the three of them had cleaned up the kitchen in perfect harmony. He pretended that it was his kitchen and that Jeanette was his wife and his mother-in-law had come for a visit. It was only after they had left to go for a drive into the country that Jeanette had tensed—gone all uptight. He wracked his brain trying to figure out why. He never knew her to be moody or even coy so what was wrong now?

Not wanting to frighten her but determined to correct whatever was wrong he leaned over and kissed her lightly, almost fleetingly on the lips, pushing her hair back from her face at the same time.

The tender gesture was too much for Jeanette. Suddenly the floodgates opened and she was sobbing uncontrollably. Now he held her in his arms, literally in his lap and he let her cry it out. No sense in trying to talk. She was far too incoherent to make sense now.

Quite sometime later Jeanette was able to master her emotions and though she was now dry-eyed she felt like a fool. She had left the house without her purse and didn't have a handkerchief or Kleenex on her. Dan had used his own handkerchief to dry her eyes and clean her face.

"Feeling better?"

"Oh Dan, I'm so ashamed. I don't know what came over me. I never cry. Why, I never cried even when my husband passed away. The tears just wouldn't come. Everyone thought I was so strong."

"Seems to me you've had this bottled up inside you for a long time. In fact, far too long a time. Now it's out, and you'll be better for it."

"I don't know. Now I feel vulnerable. My tightly constructed shell has been cracked. You put that chink in my armor. You've awakened me to a need, a desire, that I was so sure was long since dead."

"Good! Good! Good! I'm glad." And this time when he kissed her he took his time. She clung to him letting him possess her lips, her body, her mind. Her own passion and need matched his and there was no stopping it.

It was so long since she had let herself love, be loved. Often she thought about it. Sometime she wondered if she had turned into a frozen prune, unable to love. She had learned to live without sex long before her husband died and indeed no one had turned her on since, until now.

Finally awareness of where she was and what was taking place began to seep through her consciousness. She felt no shame nor remorse. In fact she wanted desperately to spend the rest of the night in Dan's arms. However, common sense told her she must be getting back. Her mother would be worried. She could not see what time it was but guessed it could be two or three A.M. It had been hours since they left the house for a little drive. Mary would not wait up for them but Jeanette knew she would lie in bed awake until she heard her come in.

Straightening up and smoothing down her rumpled clothing she asked Dan to take her home. As he maneuvered the car down the little country road onto the highway she fought for control of her emotions once again. She would have spoken but Dan immediately sensed what she might want to say.

"Don't dare say what I think you want to say. And don't you dare apologize or expect me to. I love you darling. You know that." It wasn't a question. It was a flat-out statement.

"Oh, I do hate to think about leaving in the morning. This is the first year Mom has asked me to stay, almost begged me in fact. She doesn't want me to go back at all."

"Leave? Surely you aren't thinking of going back to Arizona now. Listen woman, no way I am going to let you go now."

"I have to go back. I have a job, a very good job that it has taken me years to work up to. My home and family's there."

"I can't let you go."

"Please Dan, be reasonable. I'm leaving in the morning. In three days I must be back at my desk. I've already stayed an extra day longer than I usually do. Oh my dear, please try to understand."

Now they were at Mary's driveway. Jeanette had her hand on the door handle and would have jumped out but Dan reached across stopping her.

"Damnit, sweetheart, we have to talk. This matter isn't settled by a long shot."

"Not now, luv. I am so tired and befuddled I can't think straight. I hope to be packed and loaded and ready to leave by seven A.M. I'll stop by your place and fuel up for the trip. I want to be way down the line into Oklahoma by nightfall. Okay?"

"No it's not okay. But I suppose you'd better go in now. You'll need some rest if you're hell-bent on leaving tomorrow. And I'm warning you lady, you'd better stop by in the morning."

"I will, I promise!" And after a quick good-night kiss she was out the door and in the house.

Chapter 10

On the very day she should have been up early, completing her preparations for leaving, Jeanette had to oversleep. She really had been exhausted and was asleep last night as soon as she had lain down.

Mary figured that something was brewing between Jeanette and her old flame but didn't want to pry or seem nosy. She wouldn't ask questions but she would certainly keep her eyes and ears open.

Jeanette looked tired this morning. She had that exhausted, spent appearance, even though she had slept until nine A.M. Mary had not heard her come in last night but she knew it was late–after midnight at least.

"Are you sure you want to leave today?"

"Yes, Mother! I must go. I should have been on the road already. I wish you had called me earlier."

"Honey, you look like death warmed over. You need more rest before starting that long trip. And I don't like the idea of you traveling across country alone. You will call me as soon as you get home?"

"Don't I always?"

"Well I won't rest easy until I get your call."

Mary had insisted on Jeanette eating bacon and eggs and hot oatmeal for breakfast. She was pleased to see her spreading jelly on her second piece of toast. That girl needed some more meat on her bones. She was quite a coffee drinker but did not eat enough to keep a bird alive to her way of thinking.

She had packed a box of jelly and jams and filled a sack of yams for her to take home. Audrey had given her a sack of river hickory nuts (the large variety) and although they were last year's crop, had assured her they were still good. It was too early for this year's harvest. Lee said the squirrels were taking quite a toll on this year's crop of nuts.

Audrey had also boxed up several jars of pickles and Jeanette had loaded the camper's every niche and cranny to evenly arrange the weight. She had tied doors shut so nothing would be coming loose and rolling around during travel.

It was ten thirty when she kissed her mother good-bye and backed out of the drive. She was starting out three hours later than she had hoped to. Mary stood on the sidewalk in front of her house, waving good-bye with tears rolling down her cheeks. She always cried when Jeanette left and prayed for her safe journey home. Although Mary never knew it, Jeanette cried too. When in years past and she traveled with her husband and children she would cry when leaving and couldn't control the tears until they would be halfway to Kansas City. Ed never scolded her for letting the tears flow. He understood. He was leaving his folks too and a lump always formed in his own throat. He would be close to tears himself at times. It would be a year before they could return. There never had been any question where to spend vacations.

Jeanette drove out of town with her thoughts all in turmoil. She had promised to stop in Queen City but she dreaded the meeting with Dan.

Mike was manning the pumps when she pulled into the station. As the car he had just serviced drove off she took its place. Mike was grinning as he opened the door for her to step down.

"Fill her up?"

"Please!"

"You'd better go inside. Think Dad is about ready to send a posse out after you." Jeanette nodded and without speaking walked across the drive into the restaurant. Dan was hanging up the phone just as she walked in the door. He had a sheepish grin on his face.

"About time you got here. I had begun to wonder if you had skipped out without saying good-bye."

"And, if I had? I thought of doing just that."

"You'd have had me to reckon with, my girl. And believe me, you would not have gotten away with it. Do you know, I just now spoke to your mom on the phone. She assured me you had just left there. Set my mind to ease somewhat. You did say you planned an early start. Hell, I figured you'd be here by seven-thirty."

"Truth is, mom didn't call me and it was nine A.M. when I woke up. I was fit to be tied and would have taken off right then but she insisted on my eating a large breakfast. She didn't want me to go. It's the first time she has actually begged me to stay."

"I don't want you to go either, so don't go."

"Please don't start that again. You know I have to. Much as I would like to stay I do have obligations in Arizona and commitments that must be met."

48

"And what about me–us? You can't just drop out of my life again as suddenly as you popped back into it. This time I won't permit it. I aim to marry you darling and as soon as possible."

"Why, Dan Colton, are you proposing marriage to me?"

"I am. Please say yes."

"This has all been so sudden, so unexpected. Never did I ever consider remarrying. I don't know. Right now I feel so mixed up. Can't we just keep in touch for now and nurture our friendship without creating any big waves?"

Mike came inside then to tell Jeanette he had checked the oil as well as gassed up the truck and had pulled it out of the drive into a parking space at the side of the restaurant. He handed her the keys. He only shook his head when she asked how much she owed. Dan told her this was his treat and though she protested he still insisted on picking up the tab.

Silently, without looking at him she picked up her purse and walked outside to her truck. Dan walked beside her, holding her hand. He wanted to hold her. He knew however, that if he took her in his arms now he would not be able to let her go. He kissed her briefly, and opened the cab door.

"Call me as soon as you get there. Don't try to drive too far each day. Keep your doors locked at all times. And don't stay in the camper at night. Get a motel room. Need some money?" After reassuring him she would be quite all right and yes, she'd call him as soon as she got in, and no she didn't need money, she thanked him again for the gas and quickly started the motor. Backing out of the parking area, she blew Dan a kiss and headed for the open highway. She finally was on her way.

Chapter 11

Arizona must be the hottest place on earth. Hot and dry! Rain was badly needed. How did people live in this country before coolers and air conditioning?

Jeanette had returned home Friday afternoon, having spent two nights in motels en route. She visited with her family and rested up during the weekend. She had made her calls to her mother and to Dan as soon as she arrived home. She had had a nice trip and encountered no trouble en route. Her yard and garden had been well cared for and her houseplants properly watered. The house was as she had left it, spic and span. One of the boys had turned the air on that morning, thinking perhaps she might possibly arrive sometime that day. That was a real blessing she hadn't expected. The dining room table was covered with mail, mostly magazines and periodicals. The grandkids had been getting the daily mail for her. She had stopped the daily newspaper but had not cancelled the mail. The children were in and out every day and could attend to it.

The office staff welcomed her back with open arms. Old Mrs. Hurley even hugged her. Some of her work had been taken care of but much of it was left undone and was piled up in her work basket on her desk. The monthly reports were due out in three days and there was much to be done to assemble the figures needed to compile the final reports. At first glance she could see a week's work was awaiting her.

People kept dropping by all week long, welcoming her back, asking about her vacation. The constant interruptions were beginning to nettle Jeanette somewhat. The deadline was near and after two days she still wasn't near ready for the soft copy yet, much less the final product for mailing. The constant ringing of the phone didn't help matters. She must concentrate harder on the issue at hand. Her mind kept wandering and Dan was constantly in her thoughts, even at work.

In desperation on the afternoon of the second day Jeanette approached her boss to request overtime for herself and three other accountants for the evening. The trial balances weren't coming out right. The surest way now to find the problem was to reconstruct the entire packet from start to finish. The peace and quiet of after-hours would be conducive to clear thinking, and the accounting crew worked well together. It was the only chance they had of mailing the report out on schedule. She had never been docked for a late report in the past and did not wish to mail late at any time if it could be avoided.

Mr. Matthews granted the request and volunteered to stay and aid them in any way he could. At five-thirty he completed tallying a large stack of vouchers. He arrived at the same figure the ledger showed. One possibility of error was eliminated. Posting of vouchers to ledger had been done correctly and totals in order as taped. So far so good. Five calculators were going lickety-split. As each figure was completed Jeanette entered it in pencil to the soft copy trial balance she was reconstructing. They all worked very diligently on the business at hand. So far one computer error had been discovered. It was a small amount of $20 but the computer printout ready $200 and therefore went into the computer wrong. The card count was off by five cards–actual manual count versus card sort and machine count. Doris was tracking that down card by card against ledger entry and computer printout, line by line. What a nuisance mechanized accounting was when you needed to backtrack. The old manual system was so much simpler. Personally, Jeanette was sorry to see the system go mechanized, but she learned to deal with it. One has to move along with progress or get cut down in its path.

At six P.M. Mr. Matthews went out for sandwiches. Iris put on a fresh pot of coffee and they all took a short break. Instead of sandwiches Mr. Matthews returned with a big bucket of Kentucky Fried Chicken, french fries, and the Colonel's best coleslaw. This was his treat he insisted, in appreciation of their willingness to work overtime voluntarily in order to mail the reports out on time. All thanked him for his gracious generosity.

After all the food was eaten and most of the coffee consumed, they were right back at the task at hand. They were now out of balance $18.29. New cards had been cut to replace the missing cards and Jeanette had prepared journal vouchers to be typed to clarify adjustments made. At long last the trial balances were all in balance and ready to be typed. Doris and Iris typed while Jeanette and Mr. Matthews proofed the hard copy and Mr. Matthews signed each copy and slipped it in the appropriate envelopes for mailing. By eight-thirty P.M. they were ready to walk out the door, tired but pleased with a job well done. A nice little chunk of overtime pay would be included in their next paychecks. Doris was the section payroll keeper and she annotated the overtime on their time cards and Mr. Matthews certified them before they left. The reports were sealed in postage prepaid envelopes which Mr. Matthews would hand carry to the post office on his way home.

It had been a long day and a long evening and Jeanette was very, very tired. She was looking forward to a hot tub bath and early to bed. Before she could enter her house she heard the phone ringing. She hurried unlocking the door and reached the phone before it stopped ringing. Probably one of the kids or a neighbor.

"Hello!"

"Hi, sweetheart!"

"Dan! I just talked to you a few days ago. What are you calling now for?"

"Can't I call my girl whenever I feel like it? Just received your letter today and was homesick to hear your voice."

"Already, but it hasn't been a week yet since I left there."

"Quit your job! Resign! Retire! Sell! Rent your place out! Just come on back to me, Babe. I can't stand this distance between us."

"Believe me, tonight I'm tempted. I just got home. Worked twelve hours today. In fact it's been grueling all week."

"And I suppose you haven't eaten all day!"

"Oh, but I have. Knowing I might have to stay overtime I had ham and eggs, toast and jelly, and coffee and orange juice for breakfast. I took half an hour lunch and fixed instant soup. Then tonight the boss brought in Kentucky Fried Chicken, slaw, and fries. And of course I've guzzled coffee all day. I'm not hungry at all, but I sure am beat. Plan to relax in tub and go to bed early."

"Good! Did you get my letter? I got that roll of film developed and sent you the pictures. They all turned out good. What do you think of them?"

"I came in the back door just now and haven't had a chance to check the mailbox. Wait just a minute. I'll go right now and look. I'll be right back."

In a few seconds Jeanette was back, ripping open the letter from Dan. She hastily scanned each picture enclosed. They were all good and brought back a flood of memories as to when and where they were taken.

"Dan, they are great. Thanks so much."

"You are welcome. As you can see I have also enclosed the negatives. Turn the pictures over and you will see which ones I want prints made from. Have you told your kids about us?"

"Not yet!"

"Why not?"

"Oh Dan, give me time. Besides I haven't committed myself yet. I'm still not sure I want to remarry."

"Well, I'm sure *I* want to marry *you*. So best you get with the program lady. If I had you in my arms you'd come around I guarantee."

Laughing softly, Jeanette had to agree that in his arms she probably would agree to whatever he wanted her to do, but fortunately, she was not in his arms at the present. They talked for ten minutes and still nothing was settled between them when they hung up.

Taking the packet of mail with her Jeanette went into the bathroom and started water running in the tub. Hastily stopping to read Dan's letter she stepped out of her clothes. Getting into the tub she tore open a letter from an old friend who had once been her neighbor, but years ago moved to another state. She hadn't seen her since, but they had kept up a steady correspondence throughout the years. The four-page letter was full of news of children and grandchildren and enclosed was a small snapshot of the youngest grandchild. Now she reread the short note from Dan. She took the pictures out and looked at them again, turning each one over to see what he had written on the back. There were several he marked for reprints. The two advertisements she was not interested in and so they were pitched into the waste can in the corner. The hometown newspaper she laid aside to read later. The *Reader's Digest* she decided to thumb through while soaking in the tub. The warm water should relax her tired muscles. She was really tired and knew sleep should come quickly tonight.

Chapter 12

The days and weeks flew by so swiftly it was almost Thanksgiving time before Jeanette had a chance to catch her breath. Dan still called once a week and now and then would write a short letter. He wasn't much good at letter writing but he was always wanting her to write in addition to their phone conversations each week.

Thanksgiving day was only four days away. This was her year to have the family dinner. She was planning her menu and jotting down a list of items to buy when she did her weekly shopping. She had promised Dan she would tell the children then. He was very disgruntled she had not done so already. She herself could not give a logical explanation. She knew she loved Dan and marriage was the only sensible answer to their situation. It would be a shock to the family because no one ever expected her to remarry. She was proud of her independence and enjoyed being on her own. She never felt lonely and sad like so many of her widow friends. But there was no denying the fact that since meeting Dan again there was a need, a craving, a physical yearning for the kind of life she had once known but long since shoved in the past, a form of reawakening which frightened her, and yet stirred her emotions, to where she came alive each time she heard Dan's voice. Never could she have gotten away with putting him off so long had there not been so many miles between them. This Dan was more dynamic and self-assured than the young man she knew and loved so long ago. She knew that had she stayed in Glenwood as her mother wished her to, they would have been married in two weeks time. . . .

The week was hectic with holiday preparations going on and people taking time off work so they could journey to the home of loved ones out of town for the holiday. Jeanette took Wednesday afternoon off. She was baking mincemeat and pumpkin pies when the hone rang. Putting the last pie in the oven she wiped flour from her hands before picking up the receiver.

"Hi, Hon! What are you doing along about now? Got everything under control for tomorrow's big fling?"

"Dan, Darling! I was just thinking about you. I wish you could be here for dinner tomorrow. The whole clan will be here. And I promise I'll tell them about us."

Now I am sure glad that you are inviting me to dinner because I wouldn't like to be an uninvited guest. And I'll tell you something else little lady. I intend to see that you keep your promise about telling your kids you have a gentleman just chomping at the bit to marry you. I've loved you since your high school days and they might as well know that too. I have a financially sound business, a few thousand in the bank, and I can support you quite well without you having to work at an outside job. We are getting married Doll, and the sooner the better. You have stalled long enough. I'm at Sky Harbor Phoenix Airport. Can you come and get me or do I rent a car and seek directions to your address?"

"Dan, you're kidding. You're not really here?"

"Which will it be? Do I rent that car or will you pick me up!"

"Stay right there. I can be there in twenty minutes. Which airline did you come in on?"

It was agreed she would pick him up at the loading and unloading dock in front of American Airlines. That way she could pass right through the terminal without paying a parking toll and get back home in time to take her pies out of the oven on schedule. She never even took time to change clothes. Snatching up her purse she was out the door and starting her car in seconds.

Jeanette saw Dan before she got near enough to park. He was standing tall and straight, looking very sharp in a light blue leisure suit. Her heart did flip-flops. She pulled up beside him before he knew she was there. He had one small suitcase which would fit nicely in the trunk of her little car.

The whole process took only a few moments. Passenger and suitcase were aboard and she was already guiding the car into the traffic lanes for leaving the airport, such a busy place with holiday traffic at a peak. Even on normal days you could get snarled in traffic jams. The roads in and out were not all that clearly marked, which added to the confusion. The TV stations and newspapers were frequently airing stories and were illustrating with pictures the airport situation. It made for good reading, but the unwary visitor could easily make a wrong turn and end up somewhere other than where he wanted to go.

Dan sat beside her silently. He had brushed a brief kiss across her cheek as she opened her trunk door for him to put in his suitcase, then they were in the car and moving on. He marveled at her driving the truck. His opinion of women drivers wasn't always the greatest but here was a woman whose driving abilities he had to respect. Watching her he had to grin and got caught in the act.

"Do you know you have flour on your face?"

"Oh no!"

"Oh yes! Your hair is mussed and in that outfit you look about sixteen."

"Darling you should have told me you were coming."

"Would it have made a difference?"

"At least I would have been prepared. Certainly you wouldn't be seeing me looking like a skullery maid."

They were on the freeway now and only a short distance from home. Seeing red lights flashing up ahead Jeanette prayed that it wasn't a wreck that would block the through-traffic. Sure enough it was a wreck but only a minor one, and one lane was open for passing around it. The highway patrol was motioning traffic to move on.

Exactly forty-five minutes had expired from the time she had left until she was back on her own carport.

"Welcome to Arizona and my humble abode."

"Nice, very nice!" Dan's eyes took in the neat little house and well-kept yard.

"You take care of all this by yourself?"

"Mostly, the kids help some, but I do most of the work. I tend the flowers and garden. I have a small vegetable garden out back. The boys prune the trees and occasionally mow the lawn."

She unlocked the back door and moved aside so he could step into the kitchen. Once they were inside he reached for her but she dodged him and went straight to the oven. She had gotten back just in time. Taking the pies out and putting them on the cooling racks she had already placed on the table she felt pleased with her handiwork.

Dan had not moved and still stood in the center of the floor. As she glanced up at him she saw a scowl upon his face. He was actually frowning at her. Quickly crossing the room to his side she slipped her arms around him and stood on tiptoe to reach his mouth. Her kiss reassured him and he relaxed and as the tenseness left his body he held her tight and kissed her deeply, letting her feel his need and love for her. When he finally released her they were both a bit shaken.

Now that's more like it. I was beginning to think I might not be so welcome after all and that you cared more about your damn pies than you did me."

"Now you're being silly and more than just a little childish. Surely you aren't jealous of–pies. If this is what your attitude is going to be like then I'm not sure I want to marry you. You've been here less then five minutes and already we're squabbling. Dan I love you, but I will not be smothered. You cannot dominate my every move. If you try, you'll suffocate this beautiful feeling we have between us now."

Her little speech really set him back on his heels. Here was a strong-willed woman. No milk sop, this one. She was gentle, and oh so very sweet, but she had fire in her veins and he admired her for it.

"Honey, I'm sorry. Never meant to upset you. It's just that all I could think of on the long journey here was holding you in my arms ASAP. You whisked me away so fast from the airport I barely had time to buss your cheek. Then once inside the house you acted like you didn't want me to touch you. You got real busy, real quick, taking out those pies."

"Are you fond of burned pie crust?"

"No, can't say that I am. No doubt your family would be very disappointed if you had burned them."

Taking him by the hand she led him into the living room and over to the sofa where she sat down and pulled him down beside her. This led to another session of mutual love making and before it got out of control Jeanette pulled away and tried to stand up but he would not release her.

"How long can you stay?"

"Are you trying to run me off when I just got here?"

"There you go again. What are your plans?"

"I want to spend Thanksgiving with you and meet your family. I have reservations for the return flight on Sunday. What happens between now and then is up to you."

"You can stay here of course. But for the sake of my good name and reputation I'll invite the twins to sleep over. That way the neighbors won't talk. Fortunately, I have Friday off so we can have a little time together. I'll show you the town and perhaps Friday we can drive up to the Grand Canyon. Would you like that?"

"Yes I would. Seriously though, I want to spend as much time as possible–alone with you." Nuzzling her neck and then pulling her back into his arms he kissed her soundly once again, wishing he could pick her up and carry her off to his place in Missouri where they would live happily ever after.

"Would you like some coffee? Suppose you had supper on the plane."

"Yes, I'd like some coffee and yes I did have supper on the plane if you can call it supper. More of a snack really. One small sandwich, some potato chips, and a side dish of pudding. They sure don't overfeed you on a plane."

"Do you fly often?"

"Would you believe this is only the second time I've flown since I got out of service. I'll drive as a rule wherever I want to go. If you need to get there in a hurry, flying is the only way to go. The two years I was in the service I did some helicopter flying. Then the war ended and I got out. I had just gotten home when I met you.."

"I remember. Did you ever think about going back into service? Some did because of the job services offered. There was a lot of unemployment after the war."

"Some of my buddies re-upped for that very reason. At least they'd have a steady paycheck. I might have had I not gotten on at the factory.

"I love to travel by air. I've only flown four times in my entire life and each time was a thrill for me."

Jeanette poured the freshly made coffee into two large mugs and carried them to the kitchen round table where Dan was already sitting. She had made two loaves of bread that morning and twenty rolls. The rolls were for tomorrow. Lin had said they would fix the turkey and dressing, so this year she didn't have to worry about that. The rolls could be popped into the micro oven for a few seconds and be warm and ready to serve tomorrow.

Cutting two thick slices from one loaf she put them on two small plates and set out a butter dish and a spreading knife. She then took a small jar of fig preserves from the shelf and set it on the table also. She made all her own jams when she had any fruit to make it out of and divided it all with the kids. She was always at them to save the jars. They would save them in a box tucked away someplace but were very dilatory about returning the jars to her. She spoke about this as they ate. Dan told her she lived like a farm girl and not at all like a city girl. She liked that for it was exactly the way she felt. Being so involved with her bread and pies she had skipped lunch and now felt a bit hungry. She had rushed off to work without eating this morning and though she had quit and come home at noon she started right in on her dinner preparations. She really hadn't eaten a proper breakfast either. After a coffee refill they ate and talked for some time. Jeanette took him on a tour of the house and yard before showing him which bedroom and bath were his to use. She had three bedrooms and two baths. The twins could share the large back bedroom, after all it had two double beds in it. Lord, don't let the boys be busy tonight. They were all going to church to the Thanksgiving Eve services and she could just imagine the raised eyebrows and titter and flutter when she arrived with a strange man. She tried to explain this to Dan but he didn't seem the least upset. Anyway, best she alert her family ahead of time. Leaving Dan in front of the TV, she disappeared into her bedroom to bathe, dress, and prepare for the evening.

Chapter 13

What an exciting evening. The surprise she pulled on her kids was a real shocker. Jeanette was glad Dan was beside her to field all the questions her family threw at them. Both boys seemed to like him, at least they were courteous. They really hadn't given their blessing on the forthcoming wedding but no one voiced any objections either. Judy, Lin's wife was the only one who wished her happiness. Oh well, the others would come around, she hoped.

Little Petey was shy with Dan. Dan sure didn't make much headway there. He just wasn't used to Grandma and this stranger getting so much attention. They had purposely arrived at the church with just enough time to be seated before services began. Lin and Judy had saved seats for them. There was quite a crowd there. The parking lot outside was jammed to overflowing. They had had to park next to the wall where cars coming in late were permitted to park when all marked spaces were taken. The overflow came only at Easter, Thanksgiving, and Christmas.

After the services they lingered only a little while, visiting with friends as they moved along working their way to their parked vehicles. The music was great and the sermon was good, appropriate for the occasion. She introduced Dan to several people as her friend from Missouri. Afterwards when they were in the car Dan chided her for using the word friend instead of fiancée. She had responded that after all nothing was settled as yet. Gary and Lary were riding home with them and Jeanette felt sure that had they not been there another argument would have ensued.

Once home, Jeanette began making cocoa and slicing more bread. She set out the jelly and butter. They would have a brief snack before retiring. Lary wanted to see the late movie. It was time for the ten o'clock news. She would stay up for the news but then bid them all a good night. She had had a busy day and tomorrow would be more hectic than ever.

～～

Thanksgiving day arrived clothed in sunshine. Dan knew he would never forget this day. By noon the temperature was eighty-six degrees outside. He had played volleyball with the gang in Jeanette's back yard and had marveled at how different the weather was here than in Missouri. The weather report on last night's news said Kansas City was getting an early snow. Here roses were blooming and that red vine along the side of her house, she called it a "bougainvillea," was the prettiest thing he had ever seen. Even some houseplants were scattered about on the patio. Suddenly a cold chill ran through him as sobering thought struck him. Supposing she didn't want to leave this house, this climate, this family. Suppose she refused to marry him unless he agreed to join her here. Could he uproot his life, sell out his business and move to Arizona? Oh God! He had never thought of that. He had just assumed since she was originally from Schuyler County, it being her old home grounds as well as his, she would automatically return there upon her retirement to live out her final days. Now, after seeing her in her present domain, an environment in which she had lived for over twenty-five years, he had a uneasy feeling, clear down to the pit of his stomach. Here was a real drawback and something he hadn't counted on. Would their love be strong enough for the situation to work itself out satisfactorily for both of them?

He was seeing things now with a new perspective. He didn't want to go away and give up his business anymore than she would want to. By right he couldn't ask her to. Her children and grandchildren were here. He felt sure he could eventually persuade her to give up her job *and* her home, but leaving those kids was something else again.

The large dining table had been expanded to its full capacity. It would seat sixteen and today had ten people gathered around it. Lin had given the blessing and then taken several pictures of the beautiful and bountiful laden table as well as some of the people sitting around it. The atmosphere was friendly and everyone ate and chattered away. So much food. Dan felt at ease with these people and knew that Mike would have enjoyed being a part of this day and this family. Mike would be having dinner with his aunt and then relieving John at the station to have part of the day with his family. The station and diner were open twenty-four hours a day, seven days a week, but the garage was closed on Sunday and all legal holidays. It was surprising how many people traveled on holidays, needing gas and food.

The girls carried away the empty dinner plates and returned with smaller dessert plates and a fresh pot of coffee. There were three kinds of pie and two kinds of cake with whipped cream and a Jell-O salad. The amount of food and the drink this small band consumed at one meal was amazing.

60

By two P.M. the meal was finished. The men retired to the living room to watch the football game on TV and Jeanette was in the bedroom putting Pete down for his nap. He was tired and he was sleepy but he insisted on Grandma telling him three stories.

The girls were clearing the table and packing leftover food into smaller containers. Dan had offered to help but they only laughed and good naturedly shooed him into the other room. He really wasn't a football fan but since the others were he would join them socially. So far so good. Perhaps it would be in his best interest not to voice his opinion of football in general. He needed all the brownie points he could get from this family if he was to marry the woman he loved. Play it cool Dan and don't rock the boat unnecessarily.

At four o'clock Lin and his family departed. They were going to Judy's parents for eight o'clock family dinner there. The twins were ready for more food but Judy allowed the rest of them would eat light after a big meal at noon. Her folks were alone and never prepared big meals except on holidays or special occasions such as birthdays. They were night people, sleeping through most of the day and staying up most of the night. They were both retired now and lived their lives to suit themselves. They ate when they pleased, quite often not even bothering to cook at home, and slept when most of the neighborhood was up and about. Their tiny apartment just suited them but it was certainly crowded when the family visited.

Lin kissed his mother good-bye and said he would return the twins by eleven P.M.

At five-thirty Jeanette began to pop things into the micro to warm them up for supper. Little Petey was awake now and she wanted them to eat supper before they went home. There was so much food left–not much turkey but plenty of dressing and salads and desserts. She would fix a basket to go home with them.

Now it was seven o'clock and Dan and Jeanette were alone in the kitchen. They were doing dishes, he washing and she drying and putting away. They worked well together, almost as if they had been doing this all their lives. Their conversation was light and full of laughter as they recalled the day's events. They talked of everything except the subject uppermost in both their minds. Having finished the dishes Dan followed her outside where she hung her wet tea towels on the line, taking down the ones that were put up earlier and now dry. She tossed the dry ones in a basket in the laundry room and returned to the patio where Dan sat. He was so quiet. She leaned over and kissed him gently and he pulled her down in his lap. The kiss he gave her was sweet and filled with passion and his need for her.

"Why so pensive, luv?" Are you having second thoughts? Has my family initiation frightened you off?"

"It's been great, being with you and your family. That's a great bunch of kids, honey, a family to be proud of. I only wish it was *my* family."

"Well, it will be your family if we get married."

"If? Not when?" And he moved his head sideways, lifting her chin where she had to look at him.

"Darling, you know I do love you. Can we make a go of it? There are so many obstacles in our path."

"Sure we can make a go of it. We love each other and we'll both work at it. We're not school kids anymore, sweetheart. We can cope. I know it. Just name some of those obstacles. We'll declare war on them right now."

He tightened his hold on her, kissed her soundly, pleased and encouraged by her response and said, "Now lets have obstacle number one."

"You and I. You're domineering and I'm independent. We're both used to doing our own thing. I simply won't be *bossed* by any man, not even you. We argue now. Married we'd fight for sure. I don't think I could take much of that."

"Would you want a milksop for a husband? Surely you and your husband must have argued at times. You also must have known a love and devotion for each other. This family of yours definitely is not a product of an unhappy home life. I can promise you one thing, girl, we will have our disagreements and we may even fight a little but our days and nights of love-making will more than make up for it. With love and respect between us we'll work out any differences that arise. I'll always love you. I'll never mistreat you and you know I can support you. What more can you ask for?"

"Respect as a person. A chance to be an individual in my own right. I've always been a good wife and mother. But Dan, I need space to breathe away from family sometimes."

"I can understand that. I feel the same way. Most people do, I think. They just don't always admit it. In a good marriage man and wife encourage each other, praise, congratulate, or worry together. Drinking isn't the only marriage breaker. Some good teams are broken up from a too-jealous mate or one who smothers the other in too much 'you're mine, love-me-and-me-only-it is.' Oh yes honey. I know what you are talking about. My father was a good man but he was also a hard man. He never permitted my mother to leave the farm unless he was with her. He wouldn't let her learn to drive. Even when Sis and I were in school, Mom had no life of her own. Dad was law at our house. The only law. I never knew him to abuse Mom physically and certainly he loved her. But he smothered her with that love, almost as if he didn't trust her out of his sight. She used to take long walks on the farm, sometimes alone, sometimes with Sis and I. It was the only time she felt free. She never said so but I often wondered if she was afraid of Dad. My God honey, I don't want you to ever be afraid of me."

"You needn't worry on that score. I don't frighten easily. And I can hold my own in a pretty good fight if necessary. You ever pull rank on me and you're very apt to get a chair busted over your head."

"After which you'll need a cushion to sit on. Then we'll talk it all out of our systems and push the devil right out of our lives so we can move back into the love nest. So much for obstacle one. Next obstacle please." And he kissed her again.

It was dark and a cool breeze was blowing when they went inside. They had moved earlier from the lawn chair to the hammock to continue their talking and as she laid in his arms she was glad she had a six foot high fence around her back yard. It was a block fence that afforded privacy.

Chapter 14

Mike was at the Kansas City Airport to meet his father Sunday night. His plane was due at nine-forty. It was now ten o'clock. Might have known it'd be late.

All week long the guys at the shop kept making bets as to whether Dan got married this trip or not. Mike knew that if it was possible to do so he probably would. It was funny in a way. After all these years of avoiding women, suddenly the old man was real gone on a childhood sweetheart. What was even more strange the lady was someone he never knew existed until recently. They had always been so close and yet Dan had never shared his past much with him. He had spoken to his aunt and although she vaguely remembered Dan dating a redhead still in high school so many years ago she said she didn't know the girl at all. The romance had broken up and so far as she knew forgotten about a long time ago. Apparently having once loved her he never forgot her. Could one woman have such a hold on a man for so many years without even knowing it?

A plane was landing through the softly falling snow. The lights were coming closer as it taxied down the runway. Now it was stopping and the steps were wheeled up to the door. The door was being opened from the outside. The passengers entered a hall-like tunnel as they left the plane and proceeded on into the building. In bad weather the tunnel was always used. Tonight large snowflakes were falling but the temperature was near freezing.

Suddenly he spotted Dan. Dan was wearing a long-sleeved pullover he had never seen with matching slacks and no jacket or coat. He must have purchased some new clothes while in Arizona. And he had bought a number of new clothes before leaving for Arizona, including a new suit.

He was almost disappointed to see that he was alone. Something must have gone wrong. His father never would have left a new bride back in

Arizona. If he had gotten married he would not be returning to Missouri alone.

Now Dan was through the gate inside and spotting Mike right off he smiled broadly and walked toward his son. They grasped hands like long lost buddies, each speaking at the same time. As they moved toward the luggage claim Dan filled Mike in on the past few days. First off the weather was sure different and he told of flowers blooming in the sunshine and playing volleyball in shorts and shirt.

"Shorts! Ha! Bet that was a sight. You never wear shorts. Never knew you to own a pair."

"Well I do now. Everyone wears shorts in Arizona. Yes, even in November. Why Thanksgiving day the temperature was nearly ninety degrees. Son, you have to be there to believe it."

"If you've got a jacket or coat of some kind in that suitcase you'd better get it out and put it on. The truck is parked quite a ways from here and it as close as I could get."

Dan stepped into the men's room to change clothes, coming out a few minutes later wearing jeans, a turtleneck sweater and his Windbreaker. He had also changed his good slippers for engineer boots which he wore most of the time. Those boots went where Dan went. Now he looked like the man Mike called Dad.

It was after eleven P.M. before they reached the main highway headed home. Colder than *Billy Blue Blazes*, fortunately this old truck had a good heater. The snow was still falling but so far the windshield wiper was keeping it off so driving was not hazardous.

Dan told about his Thanksgiving, the weather in Arizona, Jeanette and her family and her home. Mike told about his Thanksgiving, about the fellows placing bets on Dan. Dan had to laugh at that. Mike couldn't stand it any longer.

"Well, now tell me the real situation, between you and Jeanette, I mean. Were you warmly or coolly received? After all, she didn't know you were coming. How did you get on with her family?"

"Son, I'm pleased to say that after all these years you are finally going to be able to call a lady mom."

"Honest? Did you get married? You're not wearing a ring. I took note of that right off."

"Not yet. She is however wearing my diamond and the matching wedding ring is in its little box in my suitcase. It's a nice set. We took our blood test Friday and next week I'm going back and we'll get married as soon as we can get the license."

"Am I invited?"

"Well of course you're invited. We'll start making arrangements tomorrow. With both of us gone at the same time for approximately a week the men will have to pull overtime. Also I'll ask Sam to fill in part-time on the pumps. He can always use the extra money and he can be trusted and depended upon."

"Dad, you're spending a lot of money aren't you? Plane trips, new clothes, jewelry, and no telling what else. Are you sure you're doing the right thing? Is it all going to be worth it?"

"Stop worrying Mike. I can afford what I've spent: eight hundred dollars for rings, another couple hundred on clothes and incidentals. Probably be four hundred dollars for plane tickets. Yes, son, it's well worth every penny."

"You must have made a good impression. You certainly made good progress in all that sunshine. She wasn't too keen to get married when she left here."

"More progress was made after the sun went down."

"Oh ho! So it's like that, eh! Well now, aren't you the old fox?"

"Be careful what you say there, young man. This lady is a decent woman and due all proper respect."

"Yes sir!"

They remained silent for some time. As they crossed the river bottom the moon reflected clearly on the water. The river had a thin sheet of ice. The snow had almost stopped falling with just a few flakes hitting the wind-shields now and then.

Mike spoke first. "We'll have to make different living arrangements, you know. Am I to continue living with you or will you two lovebirds prefer to be alone? I suppose I could batch it in the apartment."

"You know we talked about that. Jeanette wants us to all live together or at least until you decide to marry, and we decided to buy a new double-wide mobile home and set it up on that one-and-a-half-acre plot behind the shop. You remember we once discussed building a house there several years ago but never got any further than talking stage. We spent so much time at the shop you and I that all we needed was a place to sleep. We ate most of our meals in the diner. Probably could have built much cheaper years ago then now. Anyway, I've stashed enough away during the past twenty years to pay cash for a good mobile home. We won't have to worry about payments then, and high interest rates. Taxes will be cheaper too."

"Will Jeanette put her home in Arizona up for sale? You could spend winters in Arizona, and it would be nice to have a place to go to. No doubt it's a tourist mecca if weather stays as warm as you say it does all winter."

"That part we never got around to discussing at all. It's her property and whatever she wants to do is all right with me. Her kids may advise her one way or the other."

"Do you really get on with her family?"

"Sure! It got sticky a time or two, I admit. I made it clear that I was quite serious about marrying their mother. They knew I am financially sound and certainly not marrying her for her worldly goods. The twins stayed at the house at night so the neighbors wouldn't talk about her entertaining a sleep-in gentleman caller. The boys are fourteen, Gary and Lary. Her grandchildren seemed to like me. Little Pete kept his distance. He is young yet. Just a baby really. It's a nice family. We all went to church together Thanksgiving Eve and I was proud to be included in such a beautiful family group and it was such a joyous occasion. Oh, yes, son! I am glad I made the trip. You'll love being a part of a wholesome family."

"I hope so!" That's all he said but his mind was speeding on a mile a minute. Would marriage change his father? Would they lose the closeness they had always had? Would Dad get so hung up on this woman that he would neglect his business? Lots of if bridges to cross. Dad seemed sure of what he wanted and seemed to be in control of the situation. Any doubts Mike had personally he'd have to keep to himself and see how things worked out. From all appearances this romance was the best thing that ever happened to his dad. He just hoped the marriage worked out well. His dad could use some happiness in his life, that's for sure. No, he wasn't about to throw a wet blanket on his father's happiness. No way! If she made Dad happy he would be eternally grateful to this strange woman from the past who was about to become his stepmother. His thoughts turned to the upcoming wedding. Excitement began to build inside him in spite of himself.

Mike had never attended a wedding, formal or otherwise. He had never been on an airplane, and Nashville, Tennessee was the farthest he had ever been from home. He had lived in Queen City all his life. He had been to Kansas City, St. Louis, Chicago, many times, had even gone fishing in Indiana. He had never been anywhere west. Arizona could be a new adventure. Mike let his imagination run wild as he sometimes did as a boy when he'd dream of visiting places he read about. Perhaps now he could see the Grand Canyon for real. Maybe Dad and Jeanette would take a little trip to be alone and he could do some sightseeing on his own. The Grand Canyon would be the first place he'd go. Yes, he'd take some extra cash along just in case. He'd also take his camera and several packs of film. That really would thrill the guys to see pictures of the canyon that Mike had taken himself. And so his thoughts wandered on, as each man rode in silence.

In another half-hour they should be home. Dan leaned over and flicked the radio on. There was so much static he shut it off after only a few minutes. They had traveled for some time without meeting another vehicle. This was usually a heavy traveled highway. It was one-thirty in the morning. They would reach home about two A.M. He was keyed up, happy, excited, and at the same time very, very, tired.

Chapter 15

It was a clear and crisp Monday morning. The bright sun had already melted the snow that had fallen during the night. The temperature outside was thirty-two degrees, and the thin layer of ice in the cat's pan of drinking water was replaced with fresh water by John, the night man, as Mike and Dan pulled into the station. Mike parked the pickup in his allotted slot behind the station. Both men greeted John, and Mike picked up Tiger and rubbed his furry body as he held him against his coat. Tiger had been at the station about a year now and had changed from a bedraggled half-starved kitten to a beautiful orange and white striped tomcat. They never knew for sure where the cat originally came from but suspected someone had dumped him out and moved on. Some folks killed unwanted kittens, other got rid of them by taking them a long ways from home and just dumping them out along the roadside to fend for themselves.

Mike had discovered Tiger in the garbage area one wet, cold, rainy day when he took some empty oil cans out to the dumpster. Dan had enclosed a small corner of the back lot with cement blocks and here is where they kept garbage and trash, etc. Periodically they loaded up the pickup and took a load to the dump. Queen City had a city dump but no garbage disposal service. None of the small towns had such a service. People had to haul off their own trash.

The small kitten had sought shelter under the flap of a large cardboard box. The box was soggy wet but did afford some protection from the wind. Even wet and cold the kitten had spirit and fought Mike as he scooped him up. He had named him Tiger right then. He had carried him into the garage and taking a clean grease rag from the shelf, rubbed the small furry body, feet and all, until the wetness was all gone. Then he got a dish of warm milk from the diner, and spotting a carton of oil with only two cans in it, he removed the cans, threw several clean rags in the box, and then placed the bowl of warm milk and the kitten inside. He had eaten until his little sides began to swell and then promptly curled up and went to sleep. Tiger had been with them ever since and now roamed in and out of the back door at will. He hunted in the fields behind the garage more for pleasure than food. He had his own food dish inside the garage and a water dish inside and outside. When the weather was bad someone always made sure Tiger was inside before the back door was locked. He seemed to know the diner was off limits and Mike had never seen him in front or around the station where the traffic was constantly coming and going.

Now as he softly stroked the long furry back of his friend he wondered if Jeanette liked cats. In a mobile home space was limited. If the mobile was put on the back lot with surrounding yard and garden that would do away with Tiger's hunting and romping grounds. Would he stay or would he run away? John had put out fresh cat food and Mike released Tiger and grinned as the cat began immediately to partake of his breakfast without a backward glance at Mike.

"Dad, when you were at Jeanette's, did you notice any cat or dog around? Does she have a pet of any kind?"

"Come to think of it, I don't believe she does have. I didn't see any at least. No dog, cat, bird, or goldfish, nothing. Why" What made you ask?"

"Oh I was just wondering."

"You're concerned about Tiger, aren't you"

Mike nodded yes. John had left for the day. He would be back at midnight. He preferred the midnight to eight A.M. shift, which was all well and good. No one else seemed to want it and Mike or Dan himself filled in rather than to ask the other men to do so on John's night off. John was a funny little guy, a good worker and most dependable. He was, however, a real loner. His wife had died several years ago and there had been no children. John had a nice little house in Queen City just barely inside the city limits. He planted a large garden every spring and harvested many vegetables, some of which he canned or froze for winter use. He was the only man Dan knew who raised, canned, or froze his own fruits and vegetables. He would go to town only when he needed to buy something from the stores. He was friendly enough with his neighbors but never invited people in nor did he accept invites out. Dan had been in his home on numerous occasions and always it was clean as a whistle, spotless, in fact. He once helped John build on a back porch and when he wouldn't accept money John had given him a coal bucket full of very nice Irish potatoes.

Now as they sat at the counter eating their breakfast Dan wondered aloud if when they got married Jeanette would insist on feeding them before they left for work. Mike suggested perhaps she would prefer to sleep late and they could continue breakfast in the diner as usual. That was something to learn about later. It would be a learning process for all of them. Dan felt sure they would cope with any situation that may arise and he told Mike this.

"Sure, Dad! Sure!"

"What's Tom Fletcher's van doing in the garage? I didn't find a work ticket on it."

"He thinks he needs a new brake job. The right rear seems to be grabbin' some and he hears a raspin' sound like metal on metal when he hits the brake pedal. Joe had already left when he came in just at quittin' time. I was on my way to get you so told him to pull it inside and we'd check it out this morning. I didn't take time to write up a ticket. I'll do so straight away. His wife had come down in the car to pick him up."

The wedding was to take place at two P.M. in Jeanette's church on Sunday afternoon. Dan had said he and Mike would be there Friday on the three P.M. plane from Kansas City. She said she'd be there to meet them and of course they would stay at her house.

There was so much to do his mind was in a whirl but Dan knew he had to come down to earth and tend to his business. Arrangements had to be made and extra help put on to cover for them while they were away. They would be gone at least a week. Firm plans actually hadn't been made yet. The only sure thing was the wedding itself on Sunday, and there was a lot to be settled yet, of course. Thursday night when she finally agreed to marry him it was late and Friday was like a dream as they scurried from place to place. He wasn't giving her time to back out. As soon as the stores opened they were picking out rings. That Gemco was a fabulous store. It had everything–an entire department store under one roof and only one floor. They bought the rings and then wandered through the store. He even bought a sweater and slacks for himself, which Jeanette said, would look good on him. They did, too. He was pleased with his purchases. They met with the pastor who counseled them for two hours and the church was reserved for Sunday afternoon.

By eleven A.M. Monday morning Dan had contacted the men he wanted to work as fill-in while he and Mike would be gone. They had made work agreements as to wages, hours, etc. The regular crew agreed to take charge and do overtime if necessary. Joe could manage the garage fine and was trustworthy. Rhoda managed the diner most of the time anyway, turning over cash receipts and billings once a week. She even kept up the inventory and purchased any supplies needed to maintain the restaurant. No problem there. She could manage without him a few weeks if necessary. She could give money out of the cash register to any vendor need immediate pay replacing the money with the invoice. She had done it in the past and had his approval to do so anytime as needed. Rhoda was just telling him that with Mrs. Flynn leaving on Friday they would need another waitress. Dan said he would stop by the Excelsior office and put in an ad and Rhoda could interview and pick if in answer anyone should inquire. Maybe it could be filled this week and they wouldn't be left short-handed. Maye still handled the night shift alone. She had help until ten P.M. and after that seldom more than two or three people stopped by at the same time. Truckers going through ate sandwiches, pie, and lots of coffee. Still it was paying to stay open twenty-four hours. It got lonely sometimes but Maye told Dan she preferred the night shift.

Next on the agenda was to get Mike properly outfitted. He still wore his high school graduation suit but now was a good time to buy a new suit, perhaps in a light color. He'd insist that Mike take tomorrow off and go into Kirksville shopping—new suit, shirts, shorts, socks, and even new dress shoes—the works. Mike would be thirty his birthday and seemed to have no interests whatever in girls. Perhaps he was the fault of that. He never dated so Mike didn't date either. Mike was clean, personable, dressed well though not that fancy. Girls liked him. Maybe now that he was getting married and with Jeanette in the household all the time Mike would start looking around for a nice girl and settle down in a hideaway love nest of his own. He always said if he ever married he wanted comfortable quarters with a yard and a white picket fence around the yard. Dan thought he missed the big farmyard when they moved to town. They had lived in the upstairs apartment for so many years Dan never noticed Mike actually missed having a yard. When he was younger he spent a lot of time in the park just across the street. Funny, Dan was seeing a lot of things differently now that Jeanette had come back into his life.

Mike's idea of dressing up was new jeans and soft pullover shirts. Even church clothes were casual nowadays. He still wore his suit some for lodge special occasions but it was black and not exactly the proper attire for a wedding. Dan felt a wedding was extra special, especially a church wedding. He felt his wedding to Jeanette was super special and he wanted Mike to make a good impression with Jeanette's family, so both he and Mike would have to watch their manners and put their best foot forward. He almost wished the whole thing was over with and they were all back in Queen City. Just thinking about it made him nervous. He knew Mike would be on needles and pins and he prayed that Jeanette and family would help him to relax so they could all enjoy the time together. Mike could be a real do do when uptight.

There was so much to do, the day was over and already it was dark when Mike locked up the garage and headed home. Dan had left early to run some errands. He probably would already be home by the time Mike arrived. Guess he'd have to go shopping tomorrow. That would dent his bank account. Dan was paying the bills except for clothes, so that helped. Probably ought to take two hundred dollars or so in cash with him to Arizona, just so he'd have money in his pocket—real exciting weekend coming up. He was looking forward to it and he had never seen his dad so alive. Maybe this woman was taking Dad to the cleaners but somehow Mike didn't think so. She just didn't impress him as being that kind of woman. He had only met her on three different occasions and he liked her. This marriage could well be the best thing that had ever happened to them. Then again, it could turn into a nightmare. No! He would think only happy thoughts. He would block everything else out of his mind. As he headed home his mind was on warm Arizona and the joy of getting away from this cold.

Chapter 16

First thing Monday morning Jeanette had marched in to see her boss with the request for immediate retirement all neatly typed up and duly signed. His face expressed his shock as he saw what it was.

"Why, Jeanette? You said you would stay with us until old age forced you out. This is too sudden. You must have a good reason and I want to know what it is. What on earth has happened?"

"Yes, I do have a good reason. It's all right there in my retirement request if you will just take the time to read it. I'm getting married."

"What?" This time the shock was even apparent in his voice.

"Well, you needn't look and sound so shocked. Women do get married you know, even widow women."

"But–but, I wasn't aware you were even dating and now you say you are getting married. I'm surprised is all. May I ask why you can't marry and keep your job? You're not taking on another invalid, are you?"

"Dan, an invalid! No! Her husband-to-be was a far cry from being an invalid when she saw him last. She had to laugh in spite of herself and the soft, swift blush to her cheeks was not missed by the man in front of her.

"This Dan, is he a local man?"

"No! I've known him since my high school days. We got together back in Missouri when I was on vacation visiting my family. And an old flame was rekindled and now we're getting married. After all, I could have retired when I first became eligible a few years back. You would have had to replace me then. So what's the difference then and now? I can't stay because Dan owns his own business in Missouri and of course will want me to live there. I don't know yet what arrangements I'll make about my property here but I know I want to be with Dan. He spent the Thanksgiving holidays with me and my children and it was terrible sending him back Sunday alone. I was tempted to get on that plane with him."

"That's the longest speech I ever knew you to do in one breath. When is this wedding to be? Will it be here or in Missouri?"

"The wedding is Sunday, here in my church, at two-thirty in the afternoon. I haven't had time to do invitations yet, but it would please me if you and the others here could attend. There'll be only a few people from the church and some of my neighbors and of course my children and their families. Just a small church wedding. No long veil and bridesmaids. I had that one. My grandsons will usher."

"Sunday! Good God, I can't get a replacement in five days. You've got to be kidding. Please say you are pulling my leg and this is an early April fools joke?"

"Oh hush up. I've heard you say many times 'no one is indispensable.' That is why we are all cross-trained enough to fill in for each other. You can advertise for another accountant and until one is hired the staff will just have to absorb my slot. It's that simple."

"Simple eh! Damn! I could throttle you for pulling this on me. And I suppose you'll want me to congratulate you and wish you happiness as well. I am happy for you, my dear. You deserve the best. He must be quite a man to capture your heart. Do the others know yet?"

"No, I wanted you to know first. I'll tell the others straight-away. Oh, don't look so glum. You'll get by very nicely without me. You'll see."

She told the others immediately. It was some time before any work was started. Everyone was asking questions and already a shower was being planned to be held at the office Thursday during morning break. Jeanette had promised to stay until noon Friday. She couldn't work all day because she had to be at the airport before three P.M. to meet Dan and Mike's plane.

So much to do! She'd have to take inventory and decide what would be moved immediately and what could wait until later. Her wardrobe would need a going over. Linens and dishes would need to be packed. Funny, she didn't know what household items Dan already had. She didn't even know if he owned furniture or was renting his apartment furnished. No matter, all that could be cleared up later. Right now she had to clear her mind of forthcoming events and get started on that stack of invoices. As long as she was still in the accounting business she'd pull her share of the workload.

Chapter 17

Friday morning Jeanette arose with a felling of anticipation. She ate toast and drank coffee and daydreamed. Every night all week she had cleaned house, sorted drawers and closets, and now clean linens were on all the beds. The refrigerator was well stocked with a week's supply of food. She had had both the pickup and the car serviced and was ready to travel. The sun was shining, the birds were singing, the day was warm and beautiful. So why did she have this feeling of apprehension as well as joyful anticipation? She couldn't figure it out, must be new bride jitters.

As she drove toward the office complex the feeling stayed with her–her last day on the job. She had been there so long she hated to leave. Perhaps that was why she had that uneasy sensation in the gut of her stomach, a natural assumption.

Before Jeanette could put her purse away in her desk drawer Iris was telling her that Mr. Matthews wanted to see her as soon as she came in. Something was up. He had called a staff meeting for eight A.M. but wanted to speak to Jeanette first. It was seven-fifty now. The others would be coming in any minute.

That blue feeling settled over Jeanette like a wet blanket as she walked towards the manager's private office. She braced herself to hear the bad news whatever it might be, and she was sure it was bad news. She tapped lightly on the glass partition afforded Mr. Matthews some privacy and quiet from the rest of the staff.

"Come in, Jeanette." She entered and he motioned for her to be seated. He looked old and beaten and for some reason she was frightened. She had received her retirement certificate yesterday at the shower. Mr. Matthews had let the fifteen minute break extend for close to an hour for her benefit. They had given her a beautiful painting of the Arizona landscape with instructions she must take it with her to her new home. There had also been a plaque commensurating her years of service with the agency. Surely he wasn't going to try to stop her from leaving now.

"Is something wrong Mr. Matthews? You look like you've received bad news."

"Jeanette, early this morning I had a call from Fred Welsher. Marie fell last night and broke her leg. They kept her in the hospital last night and will do surgery this morning. It's a bad break and she'll be in a cast for several weeks."

"Oh how awful! Poor Marie. Do you know how it happened? Was she at home at the time?"

"I don't know any details. Fred said he'd call back later today after surgery. Any injury is bad at best but this couldn't have happened at a worse time. Marie knew about your work more than any of the others. I was counting on her, even considering promoting her in a few months to your desk and hiring another junior accountant to take her place. Now this. Maybe I'm the one who should retire. I'm getting too old to cope with these situations."

"Nonsense! Marie will be back in no time at all. On crutches, but able to do office work. You know Marie. You can't keep her down for long."

"Sure! Sure! But what am I going to do in the meantime?"

"Surely there must be a way."

"The only way I see is you must stay on at least until Marie gets back. It may be a week, two weeks, I just don't know. Please, Jeanette. I'm not asking for just me, but for the entire office. Don't leave us in this bind."

What a revolting development. Of course she'd have to stay. She owed them that much. Dan would not take this new crisis well, she knew. This marriage sure wasn't getting off to a good start. Maybe it wasn't meant to be, after all.

It was time for the staff meeting. All the others had arrived.

"All right Mr. Matthews, I'll stay until Marie gets back, but it sure isn't starting off right in a new marriage. And I still want this afternoon off. Dan and his son are coming in this afternoon and I must meet them at the airport at three o'clock."

"Thanks Jeanette. Let me talk to Dan. If he's a businessman, I'll explain the situation and I'm sure he'll understand." Jeanette thought to herself he may understand all right, but he sure wouldn't like it. He did promise her they'd cope through all situations and now he'd get his chance to prove it by living up to his promise. If he didn't agree to work with her on this, then perhaps she'd just call the whole thing off. Oh what a terrible thought.

❦

Friday morning was a cold, drizzly day. There was not a hard rain, but a fine mist that chilled one to the bone. It looked like it had settled in for the day.

Everything had gone wrong. The morning had really started off bad. Dan was in a dither for a real stint and Mike wondered if this mood would stay with him all weekend. He was certainly not a happy groom-to-be this morning.

To begin with, they were so busy last night getting their bags packed and clothes laid out to wear on the plane, and then at ten o'clock decided to do up a week's laundry so no dirty clothes would face them on their return. The Laundromat was open twenty-four hours, fortunately, and was just down the street two doors from their apartment. It was after eleven P.M. when they returned. After putting clean clothes and linens away they went to bed, and neither thought to pull the alarm. Consequently they overslept an hour.

Dan had gone to the shop to make sure last-minute arrangements were all taken care of, leaving Mike to make the beds and straighten up. The one bedroom with twin beds was a hurdle they would have to change as soon as they returned. In the meantime Mike supposed he'd sleep on the couch. No doubt they would shop immediately for their new mobile home. Mike's friend, Don, was picking them up at nine A.M. and taking them to Kansas City to the airport. It was eight-thirty now. Mike was dressed and ready Dan still hadn't returned. He still had to changes clothes and should have been back by now.

Of all times for the damn starter to act up. The truck needed a new starter but Mike had kept saying most of the time it worked all right. When it didn't he could usually fiddle with it until it did start. It had started well when he left home: now it wouldn't turn a lick. Of all the rotten luck. Slamming the door shut Dan locked the cab and went storming into the garage and picked up the phone.

When the phone rang Mike knew it was his dad. He even had a sneaking suspicion that the truck was the holdup. Sure enough, it was Dan and he really was in a snitch. Agreeing to go after him in the car, Mike hung up and reached for his raincoat.

Don came just as Dan finished dressing and they picked up the case and hurried downstairs. Dan carried his raincoat over his arm. He had on the blue leisure suit he had worn last time on the plane to Arizona.

Mike wished his dad would put his coat on. The fine mist was still coming down. If it turned cold it could turn to sleet by night. Don left town via the old highway, which was a shortcut to the freeway. It wasn't bad driving yet and he hoped he could return home before the weather turned really nasty. He said as much aloud and Dan nodded and said he hoped he did too. Mike and Don chatted merrily and Mike said he would drop him a card from Arizona and let him know how Arizona weather was. They rode in silence for some time, the only noise coming from the motor and the clicking of the windshield wipers, each man deep in his own thoughts.

Finally they arrived at the airport and Don let them out at the terminal. He was going straight back. It was getting dark and could turn into a bad storm any minute from the way it looked. Dan offered to buy his lunch but

Don said no, he had best get going. It was twelve-thirty and maybe he could reach home before it struck.

They had thirty minutes before boarding time and while Dan checked their bags and confirmed their reservations Mike looked around, taking in as many sights as he could. This airport fascinated him every time he was inside–so much activity constantly going on. This would be his first plane ride. It was raining harder now and he wondered if the planes could take off in the rain. Quite often the airport would be snowed in and flight delayed. Could the same thing happen in the rain?

The loudspeaker was announcing their flight and people were moving toward the gate. They were using the tunnel again. Dan still carried his rain-coat while Mike wore his as they walked through the tunnel into the plane. There were so many people going aboard Mike wondered if seating capacity could handle them all. It was a big plane and must be loaded to full capacity.

～～

The freeway traffic was terribly busy for a Friday afternoon. Jeanette crawled along at a snail's pace. She had left home in plenty of time, hoping to park and be inside the terminal to greet Dan and Mike. At this rate they would be standing outside before she could even get there.

Pow! Jeanette fought to keep control of her car. Now she was glad she had been going slow and was in the outside lane. Bump, bump, bump. She finally managed to pull off to the side. At least there was room here. Some parts along the freeway had no pull-off space at all.

Sure enough, it was a real blowout. She had never had a blowout before. Her tires were less than a year old. She had just had them checked and aired. She must have picked up a nail or a piece of broken glass someplace. Twice since Ed had died she had had a flat tire, but both times the tire went flat right in her own driveway overnight. That was when Lin insisted she buy new tires and she had done so immediately. Never a blowout. Now here she was stranded on the freeway and Dan's plane due any minute. What else could happen today? The tears began to roll down her checks as she opened the trunk and pulled out the jack. She was tugging at the spare tire, trying unsuc-cessfully to get it out when a pickup pulled up behind her. A tall, young man got out and taking the situation in at a glance offered his help.

Jeanette was so grateful she never even thought about being scared. Twenty minutes later she thanked him and offered to pay for his services. He declined payment and said he was glad to be of help. He had done the job so quickly and efficiently she was amazed. He had even complimented her on the good condition her spare was in, and she told him she had just had it checked that week. He had remarked so many people failed to check out their spare until they needed it only to find it low on air and dangerous to drive on.

She was now on her way once again, knowing she was late. She just hoped Dan would wait until she got there before deciding to take a taxi. If he tried to call her and got no answer he should presume she was on her way. Oh dear God, please don't let him be upset. She couldn't take much more today.

Now she was at the airport entry gate. Passing the parking lot she drove right up to the TWA terminal. Sure enough there was Mike leaning against the same post his father had leaned against just last week, but Dan was nowhere in sight. She stopped in the loading and unloading zone and called Mike's name before he noticed her.

As she opened the trunk for Mike to load the two suitcases she explained briefly her reason for being late. She wasn't prepared for the hearty laugh and frankly told Mike she saw nothing funny about a blowout on the freeway. Before Mike could answer Dan joined them and they all got into the car and she headed for home. She didn't even let Dan kiss her.

On the way home Mike chattered away like a young schoolboy. He told his dad about Jeanette's freeway blowout and Jeanette about the truck quitting on Dan that morning and delaying their departure briefly. Still they had arrived in Kansas City in time to catch their plane.

It was a bad morning all around, including the weather. Dan proclaimed that they were together now and they were going to stay together and that's all that mattered. They'd get married Sunday and live jolly well and happy ever after.

"Something the matter, honey? You haven't said a word."

"It's just that I don't know how to tell you what I must tell you."

"That bad? Honey, you can tell me anything you want to, any way you want to, just so long as it isn't I can't marry you. You're not backing out are you?"

'No! No! I'm not backing out, but *you* may want to."

"Now, that's pure nonsense and you know it. No obstacle is too high for love and perseverance to conquer. Let's have it Hon. The sooner we get it out in the open the sooner it can be dealt with."

They had pulled into the carport and Jeanette jumped out before either of the men could get out and come around to her side to open the car door for her.

"Gentlemen, welcome to my humble abode." She bowed low and with a sweeping gesture motioned them toward the door. Taking her keys she unlocked the back door off the carport into the kitchen.

"Friends and family enter through this door. Company and sales people enter by the front door. To tell the truth the front door stays locked most of the time."

They were in the tidy kitchen now. A plate of fresh-baked butter cookies was on the table. The coffeepot was set, ready to plug in. She started the coffee and invited the men to sit down. She had steaks and baked potatoes ready for the micro and a salad all ready to be tossed with the dressing. Supper would be just the three of them and she planned to serve around six P.M. Right now they could eat cookies and drink coffee and talk. Later around eight o'clock the boys and their families would stop by to bid Dan and Mike welcome.

"Help yourselves to some cookies. I just baked them this afternoon. Coffee will be ready soon.

"Sit down, woman. You're stalling again. Let's hear this dire tale you have to tell us."

Turning to Mike, Jeanette commented that one would think they had been married for forty years the way Dan read her mind.

"All right. I know you're going to be angry but you'll just have to lick your mad spot and get glad again." She paused briefly, now on the defensive.

Dan was watching her closely and caught her mood change. "Go on!"

She proceeded to relate the entire office situation, pausing only to pour their coffee. Her reason for staying on a few weeks longer was explained fully. During the telling not once did she look directly at Dan for fear she would lose her courage or worse–cry. Neither man spoke until she finished. "And there you have it gentlemen."

Mike was the first to speak. "What a lousy break."

"Dan?"

"I can't say I like it, but under the circumstances we'll just have to live with it. I know you'll feel better leaving when things are under better control than you would cutting out now. With the office facing such a dire need you wouldn't be happy leaving now. And I'll no unhappy bride this weekend. Oh, yes, I can sympathize with your manager."

"You're not mad?" And this time she did look him in the eye.

"No honey. I'm not mad. Disappointed of course. We'll have this week together and as soon as possible will set up housekeeping in our new home in Queen City. We can wait until you get there to go shopping for a new mobile home. I want you to be satisfied with what we pick. It will be your choice. Mike and I made arrangements to be away for only one week. Thought perhaps you would want to take both your vehicles back and Mike can help drive. Now I suppose you'll go back to work Monday morning, therefore every moment together will doubly be precious. And as soon as you're free to travel, I'll come back to get you."

Turning to Michael he suggested he get lost, explore the backyard or something. He wasn't waiting another minute to kiss his girl.

Mike arose and with a wide grin on his face walked out on the patio.

"Oh Dan! Dan! How I love you! I've been so scared of what your reaction would be ever since I learned of this crisis this morning." He arose and held out his arms and she willingly went into them.

Chapter 18

Saturday it was decided that instead of driving the men would fly back on the following Sunday. They all went back to the airport where Dan purchased their return tickets and made the reservations. They did a lot of sight seeing in the valley and even visited the minister to be sure all was in readiness for Sunday. Both Dan and Jeanette felt enough bad luck had passed and the rest should be smooth sailing until after the wedding at least.

Sunday was a gorgeous day. The men in their suits were uncomfortably warm and as soon as the reception was over they all went home to change into cooler clothing. Mike could not believe the temperature could actually be eighty-three degrees in early December. He had never seen anything like it.

The wedding was beautiful. The ceremony was touching and meaningful. Although Jeanette did not wear a long white gown it still was a proper and very lovely church wedding. Mike acted as best man and Jeanette's two grandsons ushered. Her daughters-in-law were her attendants. Her sons gave her away and walked down the aisle with her, one on each side.

The reception for approximately seventy-five people was held in the church social hall. The church ladies had done a fantastic and superb job on such short notice. She thanked them all personally and suggested to Dan they should leave a monetary appreciation because the church ladies received no pay during all the receptions they took care of. If a reception had been held in a hall someplace it would have cost a great deal for the services performed today. Dan agreed, and speaking privately to the minister's wife, persuaded her to accept one hundred dollars which he gave her in cash. She was very pleased and much surprised as very few of their wedding couples offered to pay for the reception even though the minister was paid extra especially the church members–which Jeanette was. For the most part a church reception was taken for granted.

There was no way they could take off for a honeymoon trip as Jeanette had to be back on the job Monday morning. She tried to apologize to Dan but he wouldn't hear of it. She was a victim of unfortunate circumstances of which she had no control. They would have the night together for this week and later when both were free to travel would take a trip somewhere.

Every morning Jeanette got up early and prepared breakfast for her two men. Each day Dan would drop her off at work and then he and Mike would explore the Phoenix area on their own. Dan wanted Mike to see the Gemco store where he had bought some things and Mike was as thrilled and impressed as Dan had been. Kansas City had some large department stores but Mike had never seen on e as big as this with as many varieties of goods for sale, including groceries.

One day they spent the entire day at the Phoenix Zoo, leaving only when it was time to go get Jeanette.

Mike enjoyed every day and Dan lived for the nights. Plans were being formulated and agreed upon. Dan would get the ground ready so the home could be set up as soon as purchased. Days flew by and Saturday came all too soon. The whole clan gathered in Encanto Park for a picnic dinner. Lary took Mike canoeing on the lake and Lary rode the paddleboat with him in the lagoon. Everyone had a good time. This was a fun-loving family that laughed a lot. Evening came and still no one wanted to go home. It was nearly dark before Lin rounded everyone up and headed them toward the parking lot.

Sunday morning Jeanette slipped out of bed early and entered the kitchen still in her nightgown and robe. She plugged in the coffeepot and took a bowl and her mixer out of the cabinet. She would make blueberry muffins for breakfast. She was beating the batter and wondering if they should all go to church or stay home when Dan came looking for her. Although she had left the bedroom quietly he had awakened as she went out the door. He stood in the kitchen doorway watching her as she poured the mix into a muffin pan. He continued to watch her as she set the pan in the oven. Then she must have sensed his eyes upon her because she turned suddenly and met his eyes with her own. It would be hard to say who moved first, suddenly she was in his arms and he was holding her tight. When they both could catch their breathe whispered, "Good Morning, Mrs. Colton," in her ear.

"Are you sure you have to leave today?"

"Are you sure you can't come with me?"

Of course to both questions the answer was yes and they both knew it.

"The coffee's done. Ready for a cup?"

"Sure."

"I wish I could go home with you darling but you know I can't. We have had a good week though despite our adversaries, don't you agree?"

"Yes, I do agree. Now promise you'll call me as soon as you find out when you can leave. I'll fly back immediately and maybe we can take the long way home. You are quite sure you want to keep the car and truck both?"

'Yes, quite sure. And the house too. This place is paid for. Anytime we want to get away from the storm weather or just get away, this a haven we can come to. The children will look after the place and do necessary upkeep as needed. I just can't make myself sell out, not now, anyway."

'You don't have to sell. You can do as you please with your property, honey. It's yours and you make the decision as to what you want to do. I want you to know that. Pick out what furnishings you want to move and we'll make proper arrangements later when the time comes to move. But for that matter you really don't need anything except your personal items. Since we're purchasing a brand new mobile home we might as well have new furniture to go with it."

"But that will cost a small fortune. I don't want you to spend all your money on me."

"It'll be a good investment, a part of our future life together. I won't go for broke. I promise you."

"Whatever you're cooking smells good. Are we going to church this morning? Mike came in and kissed Jeanette lightly on the cheek as he wished them both a good morning. The muffins were done to a golden brown and Jeanette dumped them out onto a clean cloth in a wicker basket. As she set the basket on the table she decided today she would miss church and tonight the house would seem so empty.

"Would you mind if we didn't go to church today?"

"Not really! I was just wondering what to wear." He was presently clad in slacks and a T-shirt and looked very nice. His hair was still wet from his morning shower. He wondered if maybe he should go off someplace and leave them alone, but he hated to say anything. At church he may have been able to go off with Lary and Gary after services were over. It was the most marvelous week he had ever known in his life he would be telling his friends about it over and over until they probably got sick of hearing it. He had taken six rolls of film and used it all, most of it that day at the zoo. The days had gone by so fast. Their plane took off at four o'clock and Don would be there to meet them at nine-thirty P.M. He had called Don yesterday and talked for nearly an hour. He had offered to pay for the call but Jeanette just laughed and said forget it. Yeah, he really liked this woman and had no trouble pretending she was his real mother. Never had he seen his dad so happy.

They were now at the airport. This time there was plenty of time to park and though they had quite a distance to walk there wasn't much luggage to carry. Each man carried one suitcase and Dan walked across the marking lot with his arm around Jeanette.

As always Mike was awed with the busy hurry, scurry of a big airport. It fascinated him. Dan checked their bags and they walked to their terminal with a half hour to wait. They didn't talk much but sat quietly. Mike knew the pain his dad felt having to leave her. It wasn't the homecoming they had planned. He silently prayed now that God would give his dad the necessary strength to board that plane without her. He was distracted by Jeanette suddenly jumping up and kissing Dan swiftly and blowing a kiss Mike's way. She spun around and literally ran until she was lost in the crowd. Dan never left his seat.

"Dad?"

"It's all right son. She doesn't want to see the plane leave. It won't be long until she'll be with us all the time. She's doing the right thing staying behind. I know it, but God how I hate to leave her. She is some lady." Mike nodded his agreement and just then the loudspeaker announced their flight.

Chapter 19

Brrr–surely this wasn't sunny Arizona. All week long, day and night, it continued to rain. The temperature dropped to the low sixties and even into the thirties at night–miserable weather. Some of the winter visitors were ready to pack up and go back home. Jeanette couldn't remember when it had rained so long a time without ceasing. She was glad the previous week had been warm and beautiful all week for Dan and Mike to enjoy. It had been just a little over a week since they left but it seemed a lot longer.

Driving to work through the rain Jeanette was listening to the radio. Already the Salt River had flooded its banks and Phoenix and Scottsdale were divided by the high water. Twelve crossings on the lower river were under water. One bridge was washed out. There were several accidents and rescues every day but no deaths reported yet. The TV last night had reported millions of dollars in property damage. People and businesses residing in the river belt were filing claims stating they were completely wiped out financially. Beautiful homes were in ruins. Jeanette could sympathize with them but still didn't understand why they would build in such a precarious area in the first place. She thought it was very poor planning. When the dam up river opened the release gates water came pouring down the stream faster than valley residents could move out of its way. On TV last night the six o'clock news showed pictures of the flooding. Hound Dog Acres was a community where an entire subdivision was under water. It showed people homes and furnishings badly damaged some completely ruined beyond repair. The residents were angry, some in tears. This should not have happened. Better flood protection should be regulated before those areas were sold to unsuspecting buyers. Some of the residents had flood insurance, but most did not.

A whole community of mostly mobile homes and run-down shacks was washed out completely. Because it was a low-income settlement the Governor had proposed a bill to rebuild and/or relocate the settlement in another area nearby but on higher ground. If the legislative vote went his way he'd have new or good used trailers and mobiles going up within thirty days. In the meantime the people were living hand-to-mouth, catch-as-catch-can, camping in the rain. It was a pitiful sight.

Jeanette pulled into her parking lot and drove around looking for a place to park. The only available spot open was in the corner at the far end of the lot. Looked like everyone came in early, hoping to get as close as possible to the building. She was on time but others had gotten there first. This end of the parking lot was low and water always took days to run off. With the rain going on for days the water only got deeper instead of running off.

Oh well, what would be, would be. Jeanette parked, slipped her plastic boots on over her shoes, and waded through the water to the sidewalk. The wind was so strong it nearly turned her umbrella wrong side out. What a beastly day this was turning out to be, and the weather report said they could expect more of the same.

Despite the ugly weather outside, once inside the building Jeanette began to giggle. The foyer must have had thirty to forty umbrellas open left to dry along the corridor. She slipped out of her wet boots and added her umbrella to the line-up. Poor old fat Sam entered the elevator same time she did and he spoke to her now.

"Hellava day out there!"

"You said it Sam." The door opened and each went their separate ways, Jeanette to her office and Sam to what errand he was on at the time. Sam was the building custodian and despite lugging around his heavy body he managed to go wherever he was called and do whatever needed to be done, and he kept the building neat and clean with the help of three janitorial employees.

Jeanette entered her office and was greeted with smiles from the whole crew.

"Well! You're a cheerful bunch this rainy morning. What's up?"

"You'll be cheerful too when you hear the good news. We're all happy for you. Marie called in and said she'll be returning to work Monday so you can call your husband to come and get you, anytime after this Friday that is."

"Oh that is wonderful news. Dan will be so pleased. I had thought it would go two weeks at the very least. Surely by then this rain will have stopped. Marie will be in a cast for some time yet. I'm sure. We all knew she'd be back as soon as possible. Now I feel like getting to work with gusto."

The more she thought about it the more she wanted to surprise Dan and show up unannounced. She could load up both the car and the camper and tow the car behind the camper. She could just imagine the expression on

Dan's face when she drove up to the station without warning. He could be angry because she had not called but she was hoping it would be a pleasant surprise.

She began to gather up packing boxes from various stores each night. She sorted and packed items she wanted to take with her. They would decide about furniture to be moved, if in fact any would be moved, after the new mobile home was set up and ready for occupancy. So many thing yet they were undecided about.

Lin hit the ceiling when he learned of her plans to drive the truck and tow the car. The whole family raised a ruckus, which really shocked Jeanette because it was so unexpected. Lin threatened to call Dan right away if she persisted on carrying through with her plan. He'd have Dan back here before the end of the week. He knew Dan would come immediately.

Jeanette had argued that if he didn't want her to go alone, why didn't he take a few days off and go with her. He could always fly right back. But no, it seemed he couldn't get away right now. Finally, they struck a compromise. Lin wouldn't call Dan and spoil her surprise if she'd agree to take only one vehicle. Disgusted, she finally agreed. Lord! One would think she was sixteen years old and Lin was the father instead of the son.

Thursday night Jeanette called Dan. She told him she wouldn't be home over the weekend for his Saturday night call. She didn't want him getting upset because no one answered when he called. She told him the boys and their families were going camping and they had invited her to go along. She also told him that Marie would soon be coming back to work and he said he hoped so.

Well after all she didn't actually lie about it. The kids were going camping and they had asked her to go with them. She didn't say she was actually going. If she left home Friday night and drove to Showlow it would give her a headstart Saturday morning. With good weather and driving conditions she could be in Queen City by Sunday night. She had promised to pull into a motel early in the evening without trying for excessive miles per day. Yes! That is what she would do.

Friday evening the whole crew was at her house when she got home from work, which again surprised her.

"All right gang! What's this all about? Don't you trust me to leave here with only one vehicle?"

Joey was the first to speak. "It's not that Mom. It's just all of a sudden we realized you would be gone and none of us know when you will be coming back. Maybe now you'll be coming this way on vacations instead of going to Missouri, huh? Mom, are you sure Dan wouldn't come here to live? After all, you do have your home here."

"And he has his home there–and a prosperous business. No! I wouldn't think of asking him to give that up. Really, it's not all that far. We can visit each other on special occasions each year. And there is the telephone. I'm not deserting you for Pete's sake." She picked up Petey and went on into the house, the others following.

"The truck is ready to roll. I just need to shower and change into a slack suit. Judy, you girls clean out the refrigerator and take the contents home with you. Also use my car, all of you, when you need an extra vehicle. I've already used up all the perishables but the freezer is full and each time you come by to take care of the place you might as well use something from the freezer as well. I'm leaving water and electricity on for your convenience. You did say you would keep a close eye on the place, remember? Gary and Lary will do the yard and flowers. I'll pay the twenty dollars a month."

"Mom, you don't have to pay them for that."

"I know, but I want to and the boys can use the money. Besides, Gary is the only person who knows exactly how to care for my flowers to suit me."

Everything was clean and in perfect order. She put Petey down in front of the TV, which Lary had already switched on, and went on into her bedroom to shower and change.

Chapter 20

Farewells finally over she was now moving out of town headed for Showlow. There was much kissing and some crying and she promised to call as soon as she got there, and not to try to drive too many miles a day, and to get a motel at nightfall. She promised. Yes! Yes! Yes! "And you keep your promise of not letting Dan know I'm on the way." They had all agreed, though Lin said it was against his better judgement and when he saw Dan he'd tell him so.

What with the late start it was nine-thirty by the time she reached Showlow and registered at the motel. She really was tired and hoped she could drop off to sleep right away so to be fresh for an early start in the morning.

Saturday night found Jeanette driving through Oklahoma City. She had passed seven motels with no vacancy signs. There must have been a convention or something going on. This definitely was not the tourist season for Oklahoma. She was tempted to go to an RV park. There was a very nice one at the edge of town. She would try downtown first. It would take some driving to get back on the highway to the pike but perhaps a hotel room would be quieter and undoubtedly less expensive. She remembered a little inn from years past and wondered if it was still open. She'd go there and see. It was already dark. Traffic was unusually thick for downtown. It looked like everyone was out for Saturday night on the town.

Oh joy! The inn was open and the vacancy sign lit. She hoped the small dining room hadn't closed down for the night. It used to be open from six in the morning until eight at night, seven days a week, with the cafeteria open on Sunday. Not too many vehicles were parked. She had driven nine miles off the highway. This really was a small hideaway spot and on a side road. There was no pool, but in the summertime the small yard with garden flowers blooming in a profusion of color was like an oasis in the desert.

Jeanette recognized the woman behind the counter as Mable, the owner. Mable's husband John used to be in a wheel chair. After signing in and receiving her key she stayed to chat a few minutes. Mable didn't remember Jeanette, which wasn't surprising with all the people she had seen come and go. Jeanette said it was six or seven years ago when they had last stopped at the inn overnight. They had been there twice before, once when the boys were still small. Jeanette explained she had lost her husband two years ago and had recently remarried and was now on the way to join her husband in Missouri. Mable said her husband had passed away two years ago also. She ran the inn by herself now. Next year she would be sixty-five and planned to retire. She would either hire a manager to take over or sell outright. She really hadn't decided yet which course she would take. The two women enjoyed the friendly chat.

The dining room still closed at eight but that was one hour away. Jeanette decided to go to her room and freshen up a bit. She would eat first and then bathe and settle down for the night. The bed was firm and the room was warm. The bath facilities were ample and clean. It was a cozy room.

The Will Rogers turnpike tollgate was a welcome sight. It had begun to snow and the traffic was moving slowly. What a nuisance. The truck heater kept the car warm and the windshield wipers kept the windshield clean. Visibility wasn't all that bad but the slow pace was nerve-racking and the constant stop and go was using more gas. She was glad she had filled the tanks in Oklahoma City before she left town. At this pace it would be night before she could reach her destination. At least she had seen no wrecks, so far. Everyone moved along, just at a slower rate. She had followed an eighteen-wheeler for the past hour. She figured she was safer behind the big truck and besides was using it as a windbreaker as well.

Her thermos of hot coffee was a blessing on this stretch. Now she wished she had sandwiches as well. She would stop in Joplin for a quick bite and then forge on. It was not too cold out but sure getting dark early. The snow was only flurries now, maybe it would stop entirely before dark. She should have been in Queen City by three P.M. Now it was a nearer guess at nine P.M. Never before had she made the trip in the winter by herself. She knew the chance she was taking. She just hoped it didn't get worse the farther she went.

The miles and the minutes clicked by. The closer she got to Queen City the more nervous she became. It had not stopped snowing and now was coming down really heavily. It certainly wasn't a fit night to sneak up on an unsuspecting husband. He was sure to be angry with her for her little escapade but she was hoping his gladness at having her safe in his arms would blot out his anger. At any rate she would soon be there and would just have to take what came. If he acted too ugly she would simply go on to Glenwood and stay there until he cooled off.

It was eight-thirty P.M. Sunday night when she parked on the diner side at the station. Could it be that Dan and/or Mike would be working tonight? She knew they sometimes took the night shift. It was still snowing and starting to pile up along the block wall. There were vehicles at the pumps and only one parked out back. A man and woman sat at the counter drinking coffee. They were both strangers to her.

Going inside she sat down next to a woman who promptly got up and went around behind the counter. She was a pretty woman, middle-aged, and had a dazzling smile. She turned that smile on Jeanette.

"How about a nice hot cup of coffee? Just made a fresh pot."

"That sounds wonderful. Looks like business is slow."

"Well, right now it is. A few will be dropping in after church lets out. They come and go off and on all night. You passing through?"

"No! I plan to live here in Queen City." A car pulled up to the pumps and the man zipped up his jacket and went out. Apparently this man and woman were the night attendants. She finished her coffee and paid for it and then asked for the keys to the restroom before she asked anymore questions. She didn't want to reveal her identity just yet.

Jeanette parked the truck alongside the curb beside Mike's old pickup. The inside bottom of the pickup bed was covered with snow. She would leave her overnight bag until later. If Dan acted real nasty she would leave immediately and go on to Glenwood. Now that she was here she was anxious and scared at the same time.

The apartment had a private entrance off the street. The street light was bright on that corner and Jeanette prayed the downstairs door had been left unlocked. Luck was with her. It opened when she turned the knob. She flipped the light switch and very quietly climbed the stairs. At the top she knocked lightly on the door. Her heart was pounding as loud as her knock. She could hear the TV. Again she knocked, louder this time. It was eight-fifty. She was about to turn and run away when the door opened.

Mike recognized her immediately and his face lit up. She motioned him to be silent.

"Who is it? Don't stand there holding the door open."

"Tell him it's a lonely female begging permission to spend the night."

Mike nearly cracked up laughing but he managed to relay the message. Dan came stomping out of the bedroom.

"Move on sister, you can't stay here."

"But I've come so far and it's so cold outside. I'll move on in the morning." She raised her bowed head so he could see her face. For a moment she thought he was having a heart attack. His quick intake of breath sounded like it could be his last. And then he grabbed her arm and literally pulled her across the threshold. Mike shut the door and grinned from ear to ear as he watched Dan draw her into his arms and kiss her over and over. You couldn't pry them apart with a crowbar. Finally he released her and was helping her off with her coat.

"She does seem like the friendly sort. Does this mean we can keep her? At least let her stay the night. It's dark and cold and snowy outside. Please Dad, can we keep her?"

"You bet she can stay. Lock the door so she can't get away. You just surprised the living hell out of me girl. How did you get here? And why didn't you let me know you were coming? You knew Thursday when you called me, didn't you? And he scowled at her as if he truly did intend to bodily harm her.

"Yes, I knew. I planned it as a surprise. Darling, I didn't out and out lie to you, honest. I told you the boys and their families were going camping over the weekend and had asked me to go along and that's the truth. If you remember I didn't say I was going with them though I did hope you would get the impression.

I just learned a few days ago that Marie would be back to work Monday and I would be free to leave after Friday. I had this great idea of surprising you. My original plans were to bring both truck and car and tow the car behind the camper. When the kids found out they really yelled at me. I never knew Lin to throw such a fit. They've always respected my driving capabilities and road knowledge. I couldn't understand why there was such a commotion now. They knew I was going to leave as soon as my job released me. Now all of a sudden they were against this trip.

"Lin said traipsing all over the country alone was bad enough, but heading North in the winter, pulling a car was unthinkable. He simply would not allow it. Of course telling me I can't do something is like waving a red flag in front of a bull. I jolly well told him I would do as I pleased. And then Joe said, "Lin, let's call Dan right now. Maybe he can put a stop to this craziness."

"I knew I couldn't let that happen. You would be on the next flight out and my surprise would be spoiled so, I was force to compromise. I'd still make the trip but would leave the car behind. And Lin promised not to call you if I agreed to his terms, which I did. He said he was going to tell you I left against his wishes and better judgement when he did talk to you. I promised to call as soon as I arrived. May I use your phone?"

"Sure! It's on the table in the bedroom between the beds."

"Will one of you be kind enough to bring in my overnight bag? It's in the cab floorboard on the right-hand side," and she tossed her keys to Mike. Funny, all this time she had the keys in her hand.

The phone call lasted quite a while. They all had to talk. Every weather report on TV showed the snow across Texas, Oklahoma and Missouri right in the path where she had to go. It really had them worried. Lin said he was going to wait until ten o'clock Missouri –time and if he hadn't heard from her by ten he was calling Dan. When he learned she had been driving in snow for twelve hours he told Dan she needed a good spanking and Dan had agreed.

Much, much later when they had retired for the night, Mike to the bedroom and Dan and Jeanette on the hide-a-bed in the living room, Jeanette dared to ask, "You wouldn't really hit me would you?"

Dan held her tight against him and whispered in her ear, "I am so happy to have you here that this time I'll forgive you. But if you ever pull a stunt like this on me again your fanny will get a tanning you'll long remember, and that goes for half-truths too. You savvy?"

Jeanette knew he meant what he said. She deliberately kissed him, moving her body so he would know how much she loved him. And it was music to her ears when after they had made love he whispered, "I love you, Mrs. Colton. Welcome home."